For niece & Stephanie

ROAD KILL ART AND OTHER ODDITIES

Best always &

by

happy holidays

Niles Reddick

[signature]

WHISKEY CREEK PRESS
www.whiskeycreekpress.com

Published by
WHISKEY CREEK PRESS

Whiskey Creek Press
PO Box 51052
Casper, WY 82605-1052
www.whiskeycreekpress.com

ISBN 978-1-59374-803-6

Credits

Cover Artist: Jinger Heaston
Editor: Judith Ivey

Printed in the United States of America

Dedication

This fictional story collection is dedicated to friends and relatives who inspired me to write, especially my grandparents, parents, and siblings. Special appreciation goes to my wife for her patience and encouragement and to my children for my motivation.

ACKNOWLEDGMENTS

My sincere appreciation goes to editors of journals and collections, who first published versions of my stories: Road Kill Art, *Arkansas Review: A Journal of Delta Studies*; When It's Almost Over, *The Paumanok Review*; Go Granny Go, *Muscadine Lines;* Luck, *Unusual Circumstances*; Not Harper Lee, *Pet Gazette*; Snakes, *Southern Scribe*; Following Willie, *Palo Alto Review*; Woman Thing, *Orange Willow Review*

CONTENTS

Road Kill Art

Driving home from work, I noticed some remains on the side of the road. I may not have even noticed the litter dotting the landscape had the radio not announced earlier that the Tennessee legislature was considering the Road Kill Bill, which would give the hungry Volunteers the right to pick-up, cook, and eat animals murdered by cars along the road. I slowed the vehicle from fifty-five miles per hour to thirty-five per hour to see. The obliterated carcass had once been a deer, and the only way I could really tell was because of two legs with hooves, which lay over the white line at the edge of the asphalt. The brief glimpse created a gnawing feeling to pull over and salvage what I could; however, the beeping horn from the car behind caused me to resume speed, curse, and rationalize that I had no gloves with which to collect the road kill.

My Aunt Victoria would be proud of me, I imagined, had she known I even thought about stopping for the road kill. After all, she had collected road kill a lot, not for food but art, and I believed she secretly admired those who were like her, regardless of how much. My mother, on the other hand, would say, "I knew you would turn out like her. I always said you would."

I wasn't aware of all my aunt's eccentric behaviors. I was, nevertheless, cognizant of some of her oddities. When my father's family would gather for a reunion, I remembered, everyone brought something. Fried chicken, ham, collard greens, macaroni and cheese, pumpkin pie, and fried pies are a few of the morsels which conjure orgasmic memories. My aunt brought tea—peroxide tea. I was the only relative who knew the sweetened iced tea in recycled milk jugs contained peroxide.

"Aunt Victoria," I had inquired. "How come this tea has a fizz?"

She'd half-smiled, nonverbally complimenting my perceptive abilities, cupped her hand, and whispered, "It's got peroxide in it. Don't tell nobody. Peroxide has one extra atom of oxygen. With all the pollution, we need the extra oxygen."

My inquisitive expression turned to horror. "But won't it eat the lining of the digestive tract?"

"No. It's only got a smidgen. I've been doing it for years."

"Oh," I'd responded, not really knowing what to say and watching as she waltzed across the wooden floors of the lake cabin, filling empty cups and smiling when she was complimented for her tea-making abilities. Personally, I drank Coke, feared a repeat of Jonestown, and longed for a psychology class to help me understand and alleviate my fear of inheriting her genes.

Being unchurched, divorced, and free-spirited were reasons enough for family members to label her nuts. With looks like Anne Bancroft and a personality like Auntie Mame, Aunt Victoria was surreal to me. The black sheep of my dad's family, Aunt Victoria was often lonely, I believed, because of her convictions, which were contrary to my family's Christian fundamentalism and precipitated lengthy phone calls about their sadness at her going to hell. A family member would most likely hear from Aunt Victoria lengthy sermons about the reality of Big Foot, aliens, the government cover-up of Kennedy's assassination, the untapped powers of the human psyche to time-travel and levitate, E.S.P., psychokinesis, rein-carnation, and ghosts. To contradict her was to call her a liar, resulting in ostracism till the next family reunion; then, the family member would consume the peroxide tea, compliment her, and all would be forgiven because she'd ultimately won, albeit secretly because Aunt Victoria never gloated.

I first became aware of my aunt's extensive road kill col-lection when I visited her. I was taking a psychology course with best-selling near death experience author Ray Miller, who was rather eccentric himself. I had heard stories of him burying a fortune in his yard. Nearly destitute in college, I fantasized borrowing a metal detector and shovel and digging up his money late one night. Much to my dismay, I learned the gold and silver he buried (when he feared the economy might collapse in the 1980s before the wall came down) had been dug up and cashed in when the economy improved; he'd made even more money because the day he cashed in, gold and silver hit an all time high on the stock market. Miller had enjoyed my stories of Aunt Victoria, alleviated my fear of bad genes, and felt I should record them for later.

Armed with Miller's inspiration and new batteries in my tape recorder, I had paid my aunt a visit. I knew going in about her tea, her beliefs, her personality, but I did not know of her collection. Sipping peroxide tea on her screened-in porch, I was surrounded by road kill. Deer legs were propped in corners. Clothes pinned by their wings, birds dangled from wire coat hangers hung on rusty nails sticking out from the wall. Various types of snakes, their heads missing, lay across a card table. Crisp frogs, lizards, and insects lined the baseboard, reminding me of the plastic soldiers I'd had as a child. Finally, opossum, raccoon, and skunk skins lay across the back of an Adirondack chair. Interestingly enough, nothing stank.

"You mind if I record?"

"What you gonna do with it?" my aunt asked, her eyes squinting. "I've had enough people make fun of me."

"No," I stammered. "I wouldn't do that. I might write about you one day. Plus, I want to learn."

I don't know if it was the thought of her being in print or that one relative wanted to be like her that made her point a finger toward the recorder and nod. Nearing sixty then, Aunt Victoria sat cross-legged in cut-off blue jeans, a Tweety Bird sweatshirt, and flip-flops. She lit a cigarette, tilted her head back, and blew smoke toward the ceiling.

"First, why do you collect road kill?"

"To make stuff."

"Like what?"

"Well," she said and turned toward the birds. "Once the birds are ready, I will use the feathers to make handheld fans. Dove's the newest. I was out walking the other morning and saw it on the side of the road. Must've been hit by a car. Doves aren't as fast as other birds. Anyway, I said to myself, 'If that thing is still there on my way back, I'll get it.' It was, so I knew it was meant for me to get."

"Hmmm," was all I could say. For some reason, I found her story strange. Where would the dead dove go, I wondered.

"The snake skins'll be made into belts. I cut their heads off, cleaned them, soaked them in bleach and made necklaces. I gave one to your cousin [her only child by her second husband who had abandoned them]. She was offered two thousand dollars for it in Atlanta."

"Wow," I said. "Did she sell it?"

"No, it's worth more than that," she said.

Fool, I thought. She should have sold it; there were plenty more snake heads out there.

"The deer legs I'm going to use for table legs on a coffee table. That will be an interesting sight, don't you think?"

"Yeah." I visualized family members visiting my aunt and trying to place coffee cups into saucers, and just when they were about to put the cups down, the table would move just a little to the left or right.

"I've already used a couple of raccoon skins for a toilet seat cover. I haven't decided what to do with those other skins. I don't really want to make a coat. Those [she pointed to the frogs, lizards, and insects] I ran across and thought they were different."

"Why?"

"Look at that frog. Looks like he's leaping. I came out of the drugstore and saw him on the curb. I thought he must've wanted to cross the highway, but with all the cars speeding by, he was so scared that he just had a heart attack and froze."

A memory of my mother telling me my face would stick in a contorted position suddenly became more real than ever. "That's kind of funny," I said.

She smiled, nodded. "Wanna go inside?"

My fear of insanity had somewhat subsided, being replaced with admiration for Aunt Victoria's creativity, but it was like the eye of a hurricane. I had not been inside her cottage since childhood, and when I entered, I was shocked. The impending feelings of doom resurfaced. The house was a combination flea market and antique store. Beautiful antique furniture (sofa, chairs, dining suite, and beds) decorated the cottage, yet every piece was covered with plastic or sheets. Cardboard boxes stacked to the ceiling formed walls, creating a maze-like atmosphere.

"What do you think?" My aunt asked.

"What's in the boxes?"

"Stuff I've collected over the years."

I'd hoped she would elaborate, but she didn't. "You don't think this is a fire hazard?"

"No," she said. "Come with me. I want to show you something."

We walked into the bathroom, and she pointed at the claw-foot bathtub, which looked brand new. "I redid it myself."

"I'm impressed," I said. Glancing around, I noticed a giant pickle jar, the sort one might notice on the counter of a convenience store, except this jar had no pickles. "What in the world is that?"

"Soap chips. Every time the bar of soap gets so small it's not effective, I put it in the jar."

"Why?"

"One day I might need some soap. I could melt those down and form new bars."

"Interesting," I said. We turned and headed down the hallway to the kitchen, and I felt my aunt's behavior, though a bit different, was ultimately harmless enough and certainly not worthy of the harsh judgments dished out by family members.

A hidden nook in the kitchen revealed a door. Inside, shelves on either side held bottles of various colors, shapes, and sizes.

"Here you go," my aunt said, pulling a green bottle from a shelf.

"Thanks," I said, wiping the thick dust from the bottle. "What is it?"

"Muscadine wine," she said, smiling. "I made it forty years ago. It ought to be ready to drink now. If you like it, you can come back and get more."

I wondered if the wine, too, contained peroxide. "Okay," I said, knowing her gift was also a signal that it was time for me to leave. I wanted to share my bottle and stories and wondered if Miller would like this wine. After all, he had once brought Mogen David to an academic gathering, professing it to be a fine wine. While the stiffs were horrified, I understood his humor and his frugality. Certainly, Aunt Victoria's wine would be good, and after all, it was free.

Hugging my aunt goodbye, I hopped into my vehicle. It would be a while before we would visit again, but I left with a sense of relief and hope: relief that she did not fit neatly into a psychological box; hope that I, too, might one day bend the frame of normality just a bit.

When It's Almost Over

Fantasies of skiing down mountain slopes, spraying snow, and eventually winning a gold Olympic medal, combined with a couple of Valiums, helped me board the 727 bound for Salt Lake City, Utah—my second trip on a plane. My first plane ride was with a friend in college, Chip, whose Dad owned a Cessna. Chip had cut the engine at two thousand feet and pretended we would crash. "Oh my God," he had yelled over and over. I, on the other hand, got a glimpse of what it must be like to be comatose. Then, as the plane plummeted, he turned the engine back on, laughing. I would not speak to Chip for weeks and had never been more afraid.

Even though I was excited about skiing in Salt Lake with my friend Kevin and his family, I would have stayed home and rented videos of skiing had I known my second plane ride would be worse than the first.

"Welcome to Continental Flight 322." The flight attendant smiled, extended her cupped hand, and added, "May I see your ticket?" A rectangular tag pinned to her uniform revealed her name was Audrey. Her brown eyes were clean and honest, and I wondered if she was ever afraid.

"This plane ever had any problems?"

"No," Audrey said. "Don't worry. Everything'll be fine. Is

this your first time?" She touched my shoulder.

"No." I pulled away. "Been up a couple of times," I lied and turned toward the aisle.

Audrey returned my ticket, nodding. "Your seat is about halfway down on the left."

"It's not a window seat, is it?"

"No, it's in the middle of the row."

I stumbled down the wine and sapphire diamond carpet. My duffel bag bumped seats and passengers' legs, and I said, "Excuse me" over and over till I sounded like a scratched forty-five record. I wondered why people didn't move their legs and felt if there was a crash, I would have to wade through legs and feet to get out—if I lived. An emergency door was located in the middle of the plane right next to row eighteen, and after stuffing my bag into the plastic overhead compartment, I plopped into seat B and fastened my belt. The engine was roaring, but passengers were still boarding. Still, I kept the belt fastened to be prepared; I wanted no sudden jerking surprises.

A tall, husky guy stopped at my row, shoved his Army-green bag in the compartment, and stooped. "I think I'm by the window."

"Oh," I said. "Excuse me." I unclipped the belt and turned my legs sideways, remembering football games where intoxicated fans constantly made me turn to get out. I hoped he'd been to the restroom.

He squeezed into the window seat, slid up the shade, and gazed at the runway. I wanted him to close it at take-off and keep it closed. I had no desire to see eye level clouds and would only get anxious because I could not fathom how tons of metal could go zipping across the sky. I said nothing to him, however. His seat leaned back, and the captain's voice came over the intercom, welcoming passengers to Continental and giving us details, like weather conditions and the arrival time, which we already knew.

Audrey stood straight, her dark skirt tapering off just below her knees. Her legs were covered by panty hose, giving a false impression of a tan since a six-inch run exposed milky skin. I tried to focus on her safety spiel, but the Valium had begun to work its magic, and I closed my eyes—not for long though. The plane roared and bumped down the runway. My knuckles turned a reddish-white as I gripped the seat bars. As the plane tilted heavenward, I wanted gum, but I was scared to let go and search for my Juicy Fruit. A few minutes later, the plane leveled, the roaring became a steady purr, and the seat belt sign dinged off.

"Nice takeoff," I said to the tall, husky guy.

"Yeah, I guess. Seen better."

I was bored. I had brought a book, which was in my bag, but I didn't want to get out of the seat. Though my mind raced with paranoid ideas, my body seemed paralyzed. I didn't know if it was from the Valium or from the memory of my plane ride with Chip. I thought if I carried on a conversation with this guy, it might help alleviate my fear.

"What'd you do?" I asked.

"Military," he said.

"Headed to Salt Lake to ski?"

"Nah, just going out West to get away."

"Got family there?"

"No, they're all dead."

"Gosh, I'm sorry," I said. He didn't respond. His eyes were waxen, and I didn't know what to say. I remember asking relatives how they were doing and would get dissertations on hemorrhoids, gall bladders, and viruses. I didn't want details, yet I didn't want to come across as insensitive. I felt that if I could get my legs to work, I would visit the restroom, but the seat belt sign dinged on again; the captain asked for attention and said, "Please remain in your seats as we'll be experiencing some turbulence due to a storm." Following instinct and the belief that the restroom would be the best place to be in a storm, just like in a house, I stood.

"Sir," Audrey said. "You must remain in your seat."

"I've got to go," I said. "I just can't hold it anymore."

"Well, be quick about it then." She smirked like a teacher would to a second grader.

Churchy faces scolded me as I dashed down the aisle toward the plastic unisex closet. Once inside, I bolted the door, unzipped my Levi's, and answered nature's call, but turbulence caused my aim to be off target. Knocked against the door, I sprayed the seat, which I had left down out of habit, floor, and wall. I flushed anyway, but I didn't clean the mess because the paper container was empty. I staggered back to my seat, rationalizing an airline employee somewhere was probably paid to clean-up restrooms, and if I interfered, it might result in lay-offs. I collapsed into my seat, feeling nauseous.

"You okay?" the Army guy asked.

"Yeah, I'll be all right," I slurred, feeling dizziness and dryness of mouth.

He reached into his pocket and pulled out a pack of tiny white pills. "Here, take one of these."

"What is it?"

"Dramamine. It's for motion sickness."

I popped the pill into my mouth, kept it on my tongue till my mouth was saliva-filled, and swallowed. I hoped the Dramamine and Valium combination wouldn't kill me. Of course, I felt pretty sure the plane crash would and wondered why I would want to take a pill, which would cause me to experience death sober. I closed my eyes and felt like I was riding a merry-go-round.

"Any better?"

As I opened my eyes, he appeared blurred. "I think I am."

"It's not so bad once you get used to it. I've flown for years."

"I would just as soon be dead as to have to fly again," I said.

"I've been thinking about that, too," he said.

"What do you mean?"

"I've got no family. There's no one left. I might as well end it." He looked less tall and husky all of a sudden and more like a shriveled balloon.

"Well, everybody thinks about it, but you wouldn't want to actually do it. You've got your whole life ahead of you." I tried to be reassuring amid the plane's jarring, yet I was also aware that I sounded like a talk show host trying to be a psychologist.

"See that door." His eyes focused on the escape door a few feet from our seats.

I felt a rising lump in my throat. "Uh huh."

"All I'd have to do is lift the lever and dive out."

I remembered a CNN headline about a jet bound for Hawaii where a hole had sucked people out, littering them in the Pacific still snugly fastened in their seats. I could not remember where those who had been sucked out were sitting, but I glanced around the plane. The businessman with the red power tie in front of me who was reading an investment magazine would not be all that worried about his stock, the elderly lady reading a Harlequin would not care if the fictional couple did it or how, and the annoying child who was whining to his stressed mother about a toy packed away beneath the plane in luggage would hush if he were sucked out. Ultimately, I didn't care if the Army guy killed himself or not; I didn't even know his name, but I wasn't ready to die. "Man, you don't want to do that."

"I'm a paratrooper in the Army. I jump all the time. It's easy for me. I'd just pretend I had a chute on."

I knew he was serious. I didn't want to call Audrey over, and I didn't want to cause panic among the other passengers. "If you open that door, it'll suck other people out."

He didn't respond, and like a VCR on fast forward, I scrambled for an idea and saw memories of tense times when I would change the subject to avoid emotional scenes. "What happened to your family?"

"They were in a wreck a few weeks ago. I thought this trip might help."

Manipulation had worked. I wanted to jump up, shout like a spirit-filled preacher. "How'd it happen?"

"State troopers said they hydroplaned. Dad was killed instantly, Mom died in the emergency room, and my little sister died the next day. By the time I got leave and got home, they were gone."

"My God, that's awful," I said, and I meant it. I could understand why he wanted to kill himself. I didn't imagine I could handle it if something like that happened to my family.

"What's worse," he continued, "is that I had been arguing with them about coming home for the holidays. Told them I didn't want to because they got on my nerves. I risk my life every day for this country, and when I go home, what's important is taking out the trash, who has a cold, and who in town is getting a divorce. At Christmas, they'd get upset if the bow ain't straight, if the turkey ain't done enough, or the shirt ain't the right brand. I just didn't want to go through that same old stuff. Now, I wish I would've told them how much I loved them."

"I know what you mean." Though I had not experienced anything that traumatic in my own life, I felt I could somehow relate. Many times in my own family, I had not told them I loved them, and sometimes I didn't. When my aunt gave me a miniature car for my sixteenth birthday as a joke because my parents had not bought me a car, I despised her and them. When my sister got married and had to have Christmas with her new husband's family and we had to change tradition, I was mad at her and her husband, but the good outweighs the bad even though the worst times are often the ones remembered. "I'm sure they knew you loved them," I said.

"I guess they did." He nodded, dabbing the corners of his eyes.

The seatbelt light dinged on, and the captain's voice boomed over the intercom, telling us to prepare for the landing and giving us the temperature in Salt Lake.

He leaned back in his seat. I felt drained. The landing didn't seem that bad, and when exiting the plane, Audrey told me to have a nice day. I wanted to tell her about the suicidal guy and how many might have died. In the bustle of leaving, I lost sight of the tall, husky Army guy and wondered why we never exchanged names and addresses. I saw my friend Kevin waiting. We shook hands, and he asked about the flight. "It was all right," I said, "but before we go, I want to check on rental car prices for the trip home."

Boys Will Be Boys

Career oriented and in our mid thirties, my wife and I have struggled with whether to have children. I have two nieces and two nephews; she has one niece and one nephew. Long distance telephone calls and frequent visits pacify our desire for a while, but the subject inevitably arises.

"Who's going to keep the child for us?" my wife asked as if we already have one on the way.

"Some day care place," I said, knowing part of her would like to stay home but also knowing we could not financially survive on my salary.

"I don't know if I could trust them," she said.

I shrugged. If we lived closer to our families, there would be relatives galore who would keep a child for us, but then, there's another dilemma: Knowing relatives' pitfalls does not necessarily make the decision of leaving a child with them make us feel more comfortable. "Well, most of them have video cameras, and you can log on and see the kid."

"Yeah, I guess so." Julia flipped the pages of *Southern Living*, and I went out to smoke a cigar. She knew where I was going before I went out. "If you don't quit those cigars, you'll be dead and won't even get to see the child graduate from high school."

"I know," I said. I also knew death could come from something else, anytime, and I stepped onto the deck, lit the cigar, and wondered if we had a child and we died, who'd get our child. As I puffed, I remembered how proud I was for giving up cigarettes cold turkey. Then, we had visited Brandon and Deena, my brother and his wife, in Atlanta, and he was smoking cigars. I smoked one and was right back where I started.

My neighbor's son Quinn waved and yelled "Hey." I waved back, exhaling smoke and worrying that my smoking might influence him. He scurried across the driveway. "Know what?" His big brown eyes opened wide. They were clear and sparkled, and I wondered if my eyes were like that when I was five. I knew mine were bloodshot now.

"What?"

"I like your dog, but I don't like my dog." He shook his head back and forth.

"Why not?"

"My dog jumps on me and tries to bite me." He put his hands in his pockets, stiffened his arms, and turned full circle like a robot.

"That's because Macy [his dog] is just a puppy. When she gets bigger, she won't do that."

"Oh. Is Harper Lee [my dog] a puppy?"

"No, she's old, but when she was a puppy like Macy, she liked to jump on me."

Quinn snickered and scurried back across the driveway into his yard. He paused and stared at Macy. I flipped my cigar into the yard and decided to go to the store and buy some more cigars. My wife rolled her eyes when I told her where I was going. When I got into my Jeep, I noticed what I thought was a hole in the side canvas window. I decided it was my imagination and drove on to the store. When I parked, though, I checked just to make sure it was my imagination, and to my horror, I discovered it was real. First, there was a puncture wound, followed by a zigzag line about a foot long.

I spun out of the parking lot, heading for the Jeep dealership. I was wondering who had vandalized my Jeep, how much a replacement window will cost, and how I'll find the person and approach him about paying for the window. I also wondered if Quinn or his friend Nikolay, who lives behind us, cut the window.

I screeched into the dealership; the parts manager keyed the information into his computer and said solemnly, "It'll be $139.95. Want me to order it?"

"No." I turned to walk out and mumbled, "Thanks." The parts manager nodded. I remembered getting a Jeep parts catalogue in the mail, and I resolved to look up the cost of a replacement window and see if I can get a better deal.

When I got home, I was still mad, my heartbeat was rapid, and my head was beginning to throb. Quinn was riding his red bike with training wheels up and down the driveway. I told myself to be nice because I honestly didn't think he did it. His parents and his four sisters were good people.

"Hey, Quinn." I slammed my door.

"Hey," he said, continuing to ride.

"Did you see anybody mess with my Jeep?"

"No." He giggled and ran inside.

I was left standing there, asking myself what in the world could be so funny. I had a horrible thought, one that entered consciousness and quickly moved to the unconscious. I had seen *Children of the Corn* and a verse I heard in church about wolves in sheep's clothing came to mind. I dismissed the imagery, reinforcing my belief a child as sweet as Quinn with good parents would not, could not have cut my window. My attention then turned toward his playmate, Nikolay, the child of Russian immigrants, who I had heard was frequently seen deviantly roaming the neighborhood, but before I could approach his parents, I needed proof.

I walked inside and told Julia. I wanted to call the police. The presence of a police car would cause the neighborhood to be abuzz with speculation, and word would spread quickly to all parents. "Don't call the police," she said. "It won't cost that much for Christ's sake; it's plastic."

"It costs about $140.00, and the window is canvas with plastic," I corrected.

"Whatever." She rolled her eyes. "Just go talk to Quinn's parents, but I'll bet your insurance will cover it."

"The deductible is $250, so it won't cover it. Anyway, I'm too upset right now." The sun was setting, and I've always been better at accomplishing tasks early in the morning. "I'll do it tomorrow."

All night, I dreamed of children trying to kill my dog and burn down my house. When I finally get up, I am more tired than when I went to bed. I drank some coffee and smoked a cigar, and I saw Quinn's dad taking out the trash. "Morning," I said.

"Good morning."

"I've got a question for you," I said. He walked across the driveway.

"Yesterday, I noticed my Jeep window was cut. I think

the Russian boy did it. You mind seeing if Quinn noticed anything?"

"I sure am sorry. I'll definitely see what I can find out."

"I 'preciate it."

"Anytime." He walked back toward his house, focused and ready to work on some project or another, and I felt envious. When it came to projects, I was all thumbs. Once, my sister Rachel had asked me to hang an interior door for her before her husband Rob came home. I finished hanging it about the time he got home from work. The door would not close because it rose above the frame about ten inches.

I plopped in a chair and closed my eyes. In about thirty minutes, I heard a light knocking at the door. I jumped up and saw it was Quinn and his parents.

"Hey," I said.

"Why don't you explain what happened to his Jeep," Quinn's dad said.

Quinn hung his head and kicked at the floor mat. "Nikolay cut the window."

"Why?" I asked.

"Because the knife wouldn't go through your tires," he mumbled.

I looked at Quinn's parents, and they looked frustrated. "Why did he do it, Quinn?"

"He thought it was cool." Quinn looked up at me. "I know that's wrong. He's going to be on restriction for life."

"Where'd he get a knife?" I asked.

Stacey, Quinn's mom, said, "We thought he got it out of our garage, but apparently he had a box cutter he brought from home."

"They could really get hurt or something," I said.

"Yeah, we could get cut and blood and stuff would be everywhere," Quinn said.

We all sort of chuckled. "Thanks for telling me the truth," I told Quinn.

I looked at his parents. "I guess I'll go over there to their house and talk to Nikolay's parents."

Julia didn't want to go, but she did, although she sat in the Jeep while I spoke with Nikolay's parents in the driveway.

His parents were animated. While his father flung his arms about, his mother clutched her chest, looking up at the sky. It was clear the father didn't want to believe his son could do that. He indicated it could have been Quinn, who might be lying. I wanted to tell him he was an idiot and ask him why his boy ran wild without supervision. It was difficult to understand their broken English, but his father told me the boy was not home, he would talk to him, and he would call me later in the evening. I was extremely nervous, my pulse was rapid, and I was thrilled when it was over. Call it intuition, call it preconceived notions about those from another country usurping American benefits, but I was convinced Nikolay had done the deed. Not only did I want restitution for my Jeep window, I wanted the whole family deported.

That night, Julia and I went out to dinner at Manuel's, a Cajun restaurant. As we devoured the spicy catfish fillets and listened to the live band, Julia tried to calm me.

"You know, boys will be boys. Surely, you must've done something when you were a kid."

"I never cut nobody's window. And I didn't try to cut tires."

"What did you do?"

"We cut a lizard's tail off once to see it jump around by

itself. I dared a friend of mine to eat dog crap, and he did and got really sick. I threw rocks at cars. And each time I did something, I got caught, and my parents gave me a whipping." As the memories arrived, so did the feeling that what goes around comes around, and I felt calmer.

When we got home, there was a message from Nikolay's father. I returned his call, and he was very apologetic. Nikolay had cut the window. His father wanted to bring him over to apologize the next day, and I told him that would be fine.

Julia and I had been painting when the doorbell rang. Nikolay and his father walked in, and we all sat down.

"Tell him," his father said.

Nikolay stared at the carpet. His hair was damp and had been neatly combed, and his outfit was pressed. "I'm sorry I cut your window," he said with tears falling from his eyes.

Suddenly a lump was in my throat. I did not see him like one of the kids from *Children of the Corn*, and I did not think he and his family should be deported.

"Go on," his father said. "Give it to him."

Nikolay presented me with a metal box that had zoo animals painted all over it. I took it from him, opened it. Inside were coins and varying amounts of dollars.

"He'd been saving for a puppy for over a year and wanted you to have this to pay for the window. It was his idea."

"Really?" I felt an onslaught of tears welling in my eyes.

I glanced sideways at Julia who mouthed, "Give it back."

I handed the box back to him. "Nikolay, I do not want your money. You must not play with any sort of knife. You could get hurt." Then to his dad, I said. "That's really the point here." The boy took the box from me, and we said goodbye.

When the door was closed, Julia told me she was proud of me for giving the money back. "You didn't want to keep it, did you?"

"Actually, I did."

Julia shook her head and walked away. Part of me, though, did want to keep the money. If I had kept it, I would have had most of my window paid for, and I would not have to listen to Nikolay's new puppy yelping all night long.

Christmas Presents

My thirty-seventh Christmas had come to an end. The four hundred and fifty mile drive home was quick, done in a record six and a half hours, and aside from my thirty-seven-year-old back aching, it felt good to pull into the garage and see the house had not burned or been burglarized. Except for a slight cold, I felt a sense of relief, maybe that Christmas was over, maybe that the house was still there (I actually have the irrational belief that worrying about things will make them not come true.), or maybe that I had given more than I had received. My wife was the lucky recipient of my generosity— a string of pearls, pearl and diamond ring, and pearl earrings. Okay, maybe it wasn't so much generosity as it was I didn't know what else to get, and I had liked the senior citizen salesperson at the jewelry store who convinced me in her old South accent that the real saltwater pearls were better than the freshwater pearls and that people of culture might recognize the cheap ones if I bought them. I, on the other hand, was the lucky recipient of new shoes, which so far have not been broken in enough to soothe my thirty-seven-year-old feet.

Once I unpacked and started a load of laundry, I went through what I call the grab bag of stuff from my parents. The

Home Depot gift certificate was the most valuable of the gifts from a monetary standpoint. The book of recipes from my mother was the best. She, along with my sister-in-law Sandi, had compiled all of my mother's recipes, except, of course, everyone's favorites that Mom had never written down.

The most interesting gifts, the free ones, were those tossed in the bag by my dad: a deck of cards advertising a car dealer, pencils and pens from various businesses, and four calendars of different shapes and sizes from different businesses. My mother, my wife, and my siblings and their spouses scoff at these free gifts, but I don't. Maybe it's because I recognize that it's a lot of trouble to go around to different businesses and get free stuff, maybe because it's better to give than to receive regardless of what is being given—you know the old it's the thought that counts thing—or maybe it's because I do it, too, and people tend to click with those who have the same sorts of ideas and notions.

My relatives, friends, and coworkers have called me cheap and tight, but I prefer frugal over these terms. Last year, I was able to give everyone a free bottle of mouthwash. The mouthwash had been donated to a veterans' home, but since it was eighty percent alcohol, they couldn't have it, and it was going to be trashed. This year, I gave books from an overstock of hotel supplies (not the Gideon Bible, if that's what anyone is thinking) and calendars from the local dry-cleaner. I went through the trouble of wrapping everything and putting bows on it, and inevitably, people were excited when they opened their gifts. I, too, was excited, smiling widely and showing off my two thousand dollars worth of dental work (which was before Christmas and doesn't count in with the shoes). Of course, my coworkers, having been the recipients of last year's mouthwash, knew the books and calendars were free, but they were appreciative of the thought. And I always encourage them that if they don't like it, they can re-gift it. I have done it, and I know people do it even though most won't admit it.

I can recall two gifts in particular I received a few years back, which were the most interesting. My brother Brandon, who makes more money than anyone in my family, had drawn my name. His package to me was heavy and neatly wrapped, and the foil paper glistened under the lights. I tore into the package and immediately smelled perfume. Once the top was off of the box, I peered inside to find small bars of soap and small, plastic bottles of shampoo from every motel you can imagine. My brother had laughed, his guttural smoker's laugh. "Like it?" my brother-in-law Rob had said between laughs, "Serves him right." At first, I had been furious. When we drew names, we were supposed to spend twenty-five dollars on each other, and I knew this soap and shampoo had not cost him a dime. On the other hand and upon reflection, I knew that at that time, being in graduate school and having hardly any money whatsoever, that his gift would save me well over twenty-five dollars. And actually I probably saved more than that because I used that soap and shampoo for almost a year.

The second gift I received years ago that I will never forget was from my aunt. She had given me cloth napkins and wooden napkin ring holders. I had to ask for an explanation since I had been used to paper towels.

"Good God, they're napkins and napkin ring holders. Where've you been?"

At the time, I was in college, and I felt like if I was lucky enough to get a date, I might actually impress a girl with my high society dining ware. The gift, however, did look some-what familiar. "These are cool. Where'd you get them?"

"Off the table at the cafeteria," she had said matter-of-factly.

The good impression I might have made with a date had seemed to fade, and I had worried one might recognize the dining ware as stolen property. I wondered why it had not bothered my aunt that she stole the stuff. I figured she believed that either the cafeteria had plenty and would not miss them, or that since she had given them to someone else, it erased the thievery from her conscience.

As I dug through this year's Christmas grab bag, I decided to hide the Home Depot gift card (because my wife would buy expensive house plants, which would eventually die from her overwatering them, though that doesn't compare to her father's watering his artificial plants) and put the recipe book on the shelf with others. "Hey, do you want to take some of these calendars to your coworkers? Mine already have calendars."

"I don't think so," she said.

"Everyone needs a calendar," I said. Man, did I sound like my dad.

"Not necessarily one like those," she said. "Besides, I already gave them gifts."

"Yeah," I said. "And they weren't free either."

"You know what?" Julia asked.

"What?"

"Sometimes free isn't free. Remember last year? You spent a lot of money on your free stuff."

"I forgot," I said, admitting defeat and remembering last Christmas. A ninety-eight-year-old cousin of my dad, Leola, who had never married but had been engaged three times to men who had all died, had recently died, and my dad inherited most of her stuff. He, of course, was thrilled with his newfound treasures, and my youngest brother Josh had helped him haul the stuff to my parents' house. Though they actually hauled four truckloads, they were able to cram it all into their garage, which is where my mother parks her car. Mom's complaints fell on deaf ears, so when Christmas came, we were given bags with gift certificates and our usual free stuff. As an added bonus, Mom took us outside in the garage, threw her arms into the air and said, "Merry Christmas. Take whatever you want. Just take it."

I was thrilled, probably more so than I had been as a child when Santa had come. I had already sort of snooped around. (My sister Rachel and I have this in common, except I never opened my Christmas gifts in advance, then rewrapped them like she did.) I had also seen a few things that I might like. I had even told Julia, "I hope they'll give us some of this stuff." She had responded, "No, for God's sake; we don't have any use for this junk."

Before we left, I had loaded the car with a painted silver trunk full of Leola's mail, some confederate money, a wooden stool, a painting of my great-great grandfather, and the deed to a copper mine in Wyoming. The letters to Leola, and some to her mother, had been fascinating. I would sit up late at night and read them, imagining history. I learned about diseases, wars, poor farms, and love, not sexual love one might view on television today, but glimpses of love through innuendoes. Most of all, I learned that one shouldn't inhale the odor of antique letters since they contain dust and germs. I caught a cold that cost me two trips to the doctor and two rounds of antibiotics to alleviate. The wooden stool and painting did not cost me anything (not to date anyway), but the copper mine, which had been defunct since the late 1800s had cost me a lot of time and a small fortune in long distance charges, not only to bureaucrats in Oregon, but to many friends who I called to tell I had inherited a copper mine.

I turned to Julia. "You know they have these huge sales after Christmas. You want to go shopping?"

"No," she said. "I want to rest."

"Yeah," I said. "Maybe you're right. These thirty-seven-year-old feet hurt too much to walk around a mall."

"You're thirty-eight, not thirty-seven."

False Advertising

"Don't you have something better to do?" my wife asks, shaking her head while loading the dishwasher.

"That's not right," I say, observing her loading style.

"Then, do it yourself." She plops in a chair at the kitchen table. She likes to place the plastic cups upside down between the rungs in the top tray of the dishwasher. The result is that during the wash cycle, the plastic cups flip right side up and fill with detergent and water, which means they simply have to be re-washed—wasting time, detergent, water, and electricity. My method of placing the cups onto the rungs, then squeezing glasses and ceramic coffee mugs around them, holds them in place. Sure, the plastic cups come out bent, but they are plastic and can be reshaped.

One cup advertises the utility vehicle we want to buy, and I feel a sense of rage, remembering the flier I received in the mail from a local automobile dealership. The flier read that customers could receive up to four thousand dollars off the sticker price, zero percent financing, and one hundred percent for a trade-in. What the ad did not say was that the four thousand was only on *certain* models (the ones they couldn't sell because of the lack of safety features or the odd colors), the exemplary finance rate was reserved for those with *perfect* credit records (and who has that?), and the one hundred percent trade-in value was based on *their* perception of my vehicle (while I thought it was in "good" condition, they thought it was in "poor" condition). I had stomped away mad, the salesman waving his arms and preaching how I was still getting a deal.

I finish loading the dishwasher, turn toward her. "What I was saying was that I'm tired of this false advertisement business, and I'm gonna start calling and complaining."

"Well, do it then."

"I will," I snap, but part of me doesn't want to because I honestly believe people who answer the phones don't want to hear it and will not pass my complaint on to those who could do something about it.

"Why don't you just take a nap? You didn't get much sleep last night."

"I don't need a nap," I say, but I know she is right. I had barely slept and, if I did take a nap, I would probably feel better and forget my desire to call people and complain even though I still believe it's important.

The night before, I had been in a meeting in a city about a two-hour drive from home. All day, weathermen on the local news channels had been dramatically talking, mapping red blobs on radar, and giving instructions about the possibility of meteorological disaster. Their tactics, like sales people it seemed to me, consisted of fear and, like the general public, I was affected. A sense of trepidation pervaded my spirit, and I had not particularly wanted to attend the meeting. On the other hand, I knew how often weathermen had made forecasts which failed to materialize.

When I finally left Cookeville, the sky was a grape color, and it was raining. Once on the interstate, the wind was blowing my truck back and forth, and I could barely see the car's taillights in front of me. I was sure I appeared drunk to those behind me. I feared being blown off the road and, because the steep, mountainous road has valleys over a thousand feet below, I feared falling, tumbling, and smashing to a traumatic death. I imagined that if I lived, I would not be found for days, and by then I would have been picked clean by scavenging birds—a leftover fear from my childhood thanks to Hitchcock.

It took me over an hour and a half doing forty miles per hour to arrive at the exit. When I pulled off, I felt drained. I stopped at a convenience store, got soaked running in, bought a coffee, and sat in my truck wet and shivering while I sipped the coffee and rubbed my eyes. My radio scanned for stations, and each one it found had a disk jockey excitedly announcing weather news. I had driven through several counties, and though I had not experienced hail or a tornado, they had been reported in every county I had driven through.

The wind rocking my truck, I pulled back onto the two-lane highway, which would lead me home. Without the heavy traffic's lights on the interstate, the road was even darker. As I crept along the road, lightning flashed, and for a moment afterward, it was even more difficult to see, like when I would turn off the overhead light in a room at night and find myself bumping into furniture that I knew was there but could not see. My perception became even more altered as the wind blew shrubbery, and I imagined they were startled deer leaping in front of my truck. Each time, I slammed my foot on the brake pedal and nearly lost what little control I had.

As I topped a hill, lightning flashed. I saw clouds swirling above me, and I knew a tornado could touch down at any minute. My pulse was rapid and sweat beads dripped from my forehead. Another flash of lightning and I saw the sign: *Prepare to Meet Thy Maker*. My truck left the road, went into a ditch, came back onto the road, made a one hundred eighty degree turn, and stopped, facing in the opposite direction.

My heart pounding like a hard rock drummer and my body shaking like a coffee addict, I made a U-turn to resume traveling in the right direction. I drove even slower because I did not want to meet my maker. Furthermore, I wasn't ready to meet my maker. I promised aloud I would improve my-self—stop smoking, stop worrying about little things I can't change, become more loving to family and friends, begin vol-unteering for charities—and I imagined ways I would accomplish my new goals the rest of the way home.

The fact is, I won't change. Sure, occasionally I will think about the *Prepare to Meet Thy Maker* sign, but whenever I do, I'll get angry because of the way some ministers, like advertis-ers, use scare tactics to sway people to buy their ideas. I also feel anger, masking anxiety and dread, that one day I will find out if I should have bought the advertisement. I also feel re-lieved, even elated, that my time is not done, that somehow I won over nature.

Dishwasher finally loaded, I turn to my wife who is read-ing a magazine. "I think I'll take a nap," I say.

"You want me to wake you?"

"No, I'll get up sooner or later."

A Good Deed

Good deeds often seem not worth the trouble, so why I keep doing them is beyond me. Sitting at a stoplight, I have held up traffic behind me and allowed cars on the opposite side to turn in front of me because I've been on the other side trying to turn, not being able to due to the volume of traffic and sitting through another light. When I give the signal for the drivers to go, they speed away, sometimes waving and sometimes not. The driver behind, though, seems angry and frustrated that I have made him wait and usually blows his horn or flips me off. At some level, I feel really good that I've done a good deed. On another level, I feel persecuted by those who don't see my deed as a good one. Maybe it's a Jesus complex or something.

After I did a good deed for my cousin Raleigh and his wife Catherine, I decided that my days of doing good deeds had come to an end, and I resolved that when someone called and said, "I was wondering if you could do me a favor," I would take Nancy Reagan's slogan out of context and "just say no."

Raleigh, my first cousin on my mother's side, is four years younger than me and never lets me forget it. Of course,

I never let him forget that I inherited the "keep your hair gene as you get old," and he did not. I also remind him that I have saved a fortune by wearing a size thirty-two waist for over ten years when he has had to buy increasingly larger sizes. Our family was delighted when he married Catherine several years ago. Her family, on the other hand, had hoped for a financially better match.

Raleigh and Catherine moved around a lot because of jobs and graduate school and finally settled in Murfreesboro, where they bought a house a couple of miles from ours. Their house is in a different subdivision, but someone passing through wouldn't know that because the subdivisions simply run together and can be quite confusing. From Northfield Street, which circles the city and, incidentally, where I let people turn in front of me, the houses begin as cookie cutter vinyl/brick patio homes labeled with a brick sign "Saddlebrook." If you turn right on Saddlebrook, you go into Hanes Haven. If you go straight, you go into Ravenwood. If you turn left, you go into Indian Springs. If you go straight through Ravenwood, you go into Regency Park, then into Russell Heights, which is where Raleigh and Catherine live.

Raleigh and I are similar in the sense that when we were searching for houses, we had two specific requirements: big trees and a real fireplace. We objected to Bradford pear trees because they are indicators that a new subdivision has been constructed by underpaid Mexican migrant workers in what used to be farm fields. Though they are fast growing and a favorite of supposed landscapers, Bradford pear trees are also known to split, get hit by lightning, contract diseases, blow over in storms, and smell like rotten fish in the spring when in bloom. Raleigh and I also objected to homes with fake vinyl chimneys and gas fireplaces. We both believed that the wood burning masonry fireplace created more of a winter ambiance, like movies we watched growing up in South Georgia. In the event of an ice storm, we believed we could always burn wood when the natural gas was out and that real fireplaces were more masculine than the lazy flip-of-a-switch mentality you get with ugly gas logs with little flames shooting up. No matter how hard manufacturers try, the gas logs will never look real, nor will the flames.

When the phone rings, I always check caller ID. I pay Ma Bell a fee each month to reject anonymous calls and let me know who's calling. Most of the time, the anonymous callers get through because they can bypass Ma Bell's technology and always the callers are telemarketers, trying to sell me something I don't want or need. Life has become a war of words, and you have to be careful of what you say, how you say it, or they continue to call and sometimes sell you a service or product when you aren't even aware you have made a purchase. I recognized the number as Raleigh and Catherine.

"Hello?" I think it's silly to answer the phone this way when he knows I know who is calling to begin with.

"What's up?"

"Not much. Just scanning channels trying to find something worth watching." I think it is amazing that I pay close to fifty dollars a month for cable, get over eighty channels, and can't find anything worth watching. "What are ya'll doing?" I asked.

"Catherine's not home yet, and I've been painting."

"Sounds like fun," I sarcastically replied. Julia and I had painted some, then finally hired someone to do it because we hated it and didn't do a good job, spilling paint on the carpet and missing spots.

"You can come help if you want," Raleigh said and chuckled.

"I'd love to. Be right over." He knew I wasn't serious. I felt guilty, though, because we had been out of town when they moved into the house, and we hadn't helped them. Nor had we helped them do much of anything and having been a homeowner for only two years, I knew how badly new home-owners needed help.

"What are ya'll doing for dinner?"

"I don't know," I said. "I haven't talked to Julia, but we don't have anything thawed out to cook."

"Want to go to Cracker Barrel?"

"Sounds good to me," I said. "When Julia gets home, we'll come over." With its nostalgic and antique décor, Cracker Barrel had the wholesome, home-style, Southern cooking that Raleigh and I grew up eating, and unless we went home for a holiday or a family reunion, we normally ate pre-packaged frozen dinners or fast food because of the hectic schedules that working couples often keep.

When Julia got home from work, I told her we were going to dinner at Cracker Barrel with Raleigh and Catherine, which was fine with her. She changed clothes, and we drove over to their house. When we pulled in the driveway, I noticed the grass, in places, was nearly two feet tall.

"Good God," I told Julia. "He needs to mow. He might not even have a lawn mower."

"Why don't you come mow it for him?"

"I guess I could do that," I said. What I wanted to tell Julia was: "Why don't you mow it yourself, Miss Tell-somebody-else-what-to-do."

Raleigh and Catherine saw us pull in and came outside. They jumped into the Jetta and off we went. I asked Raleigh about his yard, and he told me he hadn't been able to buy a lawn mower—that with the down payment and closing costs he couldn't afford one just yet. I told him I'd come mow it. Usually we have to wait at Cracker Barrel, but since it was a weeknight, we got a table right away. After stuffing ourselves with the home cooking, we dropped Raleigh and Catherine off at their house and headed home.

I left work a little early the next afternoon, and though it was nearly one hundred degrees with one hundred percent humidity, I decided to drive my lawn mower to his house and mow. Equipped with a hat, sunglasses, a big jug of ice water, I pulled out of the driveway for the two-mile trek. It was interesting driving down the road on the lawn mower. I noticed people's houses, landscaping, curtains, and cars more than I ever had driving my vehicle, which was due to the turtle pace of the lawn mower. What was difficult was crossing the main road from Ravenwood to Russell Heights. A continuous onslaught of cars kept me from crossing, so I rode the white line at the edge of the asphalt, half on the road and half off the road, till I got to the entrance of Russell Heights. Then, I shot across the road, looking first but still almost getting creamed by high school students going way too fast. Leaning out the window, they yelled something, and though I couldn't hear them for the roar of the lawn mower, I suspected I knew what they'd said.

I tackled Raleigh and Catherine's front yard first because the grass there was the highest and thickest. It was like cutting hay. I had to imagine, since I've never cut hay. They also have no trees in the front, so the lack of shade and the direct sunlight in the high temperature combined with high humidity made sweat pour from my body. If I was mowing at home, I'd put the lawn mower in fourth or fifth gear and cut the grass quicker, sloppier, but I couldn't go fast in their jungle.

When I completed the front, I pulled under a redbud tree next to the driveway and cut the engine. I downed the ice water, and tilting my head back, I watched the black clouds increase and swirl. I felt the ice water might prevent a stroke or heart attack, but nothing would help me if I got hit by lightning. I imagined I would lie in the backyard being covered by bugs till Raleigh and Catherine finally got home near dusk. I knew if traffic was heavy in Nashville and it got dark, I could lie in the yard all night, and they would never know I was outside dying. It is simply amazing what we go through for other people.

I shook the images out of mind and cranked the lawn mower. The backyard was cooler because of the shade, and the grass wasn't as thick, but my heart still pounded, and my head throbbed. I couldn't breathe through my nose either. I tried to mow the ditch, but my riding mower couldn't make the incline, so I gave up that idea. I had heard of a man whose lawn mower had toppled over and killed him. Lightning, heart attack, and stroke were deaths people would grieve at a funeral: "Lord knows he was a good man," or "Taken so young," or "Always doing a good deed." Being killed by a lawn mower, in contrast, seemed undignified, and I could hear my friends: "What a dumb ass," or "If he'd bought a Snapper that wouldn't have happened," or "Julia is better off without him."

The breeze on the drive back home was nice. The clouds covered the sun. Traffic was not as heavy when I crossed Haynes, but as I darted through the subdivision, a police officer pointed at me. I waved and kept going. I pulled in the driveway, cut the ignition, and ran up the steps to the back door. I couldn't wait to get inside, where I had the air conditioning running full blast. Because of all that ice water, I also couldn't wait to use the restroom. I reached into my pockets, searching for the keys.

The sinking feeling only lasted a moment. Replaced by rage, I stomped around the deck, cursing. The dog ran into her dog house as did the neighbor's Dalmatian. All of a sudden, I *really* had to go to the bathroom, like when you're in church and don't want to get up till they are praying or singing when you won't be noticed. You feel like if you get up when the minister's into his hellfire sermon, he may thunder, "Hey you, the one who's rushing out to use the bathroom, don't you have any faith?"

Why I walked to the back door and looked in again is beyond me. I could see the keys lying neatly next to my wallet on the dining room table. I wanted to cry. I ran through a list of possibilities. First, I could bust one of the glass panes, reach through, and unlock the door. Problem is that I couldn't replace a section of the glass door. The whole thing would have to be replaced, and that would cost about two hundred dollars. Then I thought about a window, which presented another list of problems. There are storm windows screwed into the wood over the windows. I'd need a screwdriver, which was in the locked garage. I knew even if I could borrow a screwdriver and could get one of the storm windows off, the window itself would be locked because I am paranoid of a break-in. Besides, a broken window would cost over a hundred dollars to repair or replace. Though it's nice to live in an area with a booming economy, it's tough to get someone to do something at a fair price—if you can actually get someone to do something.

I knew one thing. I had to go to the restroom. I felt like someone might see me if I went into the bushes, so I held it longer. I laid on the deck, the sun beating on my face. My bladder felt like it would explode. When I could take the pain no longer, I crept into the flowerbed, stood behind a red tip, and relieved myself. As I finished, I heard my neighbor's van pulling into their driveway. They were climbing out of the van and slamming doors when I came out of the bushes.

"Hey," I said, walking toward them.

"Hey," they responded.

"Do ya'll mind if I use your phone? I'm locked out."

"Sure, come on in."

I dialed Julia's number at work. "Can you leave work now and come home? I've locked myself out."

She laughed. "Okay. Give me a few minutes."

I hung up without saying goodbye, a trait that annoyed her.

"Thanks," I said to my neighbors, Stacey and Samuel, who stepped back away from me—bothered by my stench, I assumed.

"Do you have a credit card?" Stacey asked.

"Sure," I said. "Why?"

"We could use that to get in through the side door to your garage."

"Well," I stuttered. "It's in my wallet on the dining room table, next to the keys."

"I've got a card I can use. It expires this week."

We all traipsed over to the side door, and within two minutes the door was open. I managed to shove all the junk blocking the door aside and squeeze inside. "Thanks," I said.

"Isn't it comforting to know your neighbors can break into your house?" Stacey asked.

"This time it was," I said.

Once inside, the coolness overwhelmed me. I sat and plopped my feet on the coffee table. I tried to call Julia, but didn't get an answer. She would be mad that she rushed home to find me already inside. When she did get home about thirty minutes later, she wasn't mad. Instead, she laughed.

"I can't believe you locked yourself out. That's so unlike you."

"It'll be the last time, too. I'll have a key made and hide it. I don't particularly like urinating in the bushes and having the neighbors catch me. And it's the last time I do a good deed."

"Well, I'm sure Raleigh and Catherine will appreciate it."

"Raleigh can come get the lawn mower and do it himself. I could've died out there."

"You're exaggerating."

The phone rang and since she was standing, Julia checked Caller ID. It was Raleigh, and she handed the portable phone to me.

"Hey, thanks for mowing the grass," Raleigh said.

"You're welcome."

"It must've been hot."

I told him how hot it was, how I had to ride the lawn mower through traffic, how I had locked myself out, how I had to go to the bathroom.

"I can't believe you rode the lawn mower over here. It's against the law to ride a lawn mower on city streets," he scolded.

"That would explain the policeman pointing at me," I said.

"It's a wonder he didn't chase you down and give you a ticket."

"I'm glad he didn't."

"Me, too, but I wish you would've raked up all this hay before you left," he said.

I swallowed, kept my cool, and said nothing. My guess is Raleigh was joking, but I didn't want to know it if he wasn't. He told me again how much he appreciated my good deed, and I told him he was welcome. I knew I wouldn't do it again. When we hung up, Julia placed the portable phone back on its stand.

"When are you going to mow our yard?" she asked.

"Why don't you mow it yourself Miss Tell-somebody-else-what-to-do."

Julia stomped away, and I giggled silently. I knew she would get over my sarcasm in a few minutes, and I also knew she would be more conscious of suggesting things for me to do. For the time being, I was off the hook. No good deeds. No deeds whatsoever.

Go Granny Go

Mailing bills at the Post Office is frustrating. All of a sudden, the money you have worked so hard for disappears through a little slot; you're so worried the money won't reach the creditors on time, you open the slot door again to check and make sure the envelopes didn't get stuck. I don't, however, get too depressed about it. What is more frustrating, though, are the countless cars pulling in and out of parking spaces without looking to see if anyone is behind them.

Easing my truck into the parking space, I cut the ignition and gathered the envelopes. As I walked across the lot, checking the envelopes to make sure the licked stamps hadn't come off, I almost became a permanent fixture on the parking lot, like gum, oil stains, and foodstuff birds eat. The green minivan was upon me before I noticed it, and my hand actually slapped the back door. I leaped (frog-like and awkwardly since I'm so out of shape) ten feet, all the while slowly yelling, "Daaaammmmmnnnn!" sounding like a forty-five record on the thirty-three speed. I turned to see who had it in for me. A stout woman with gray hair was reading her mail and driving. No look of regret for almost having killed me, no apology, nothing. The minivan just putted through the parking lot, leaving little puffs of smoke behind.

"Crazy old bat," I muttered, "probably works for one of my creditors." I wanted to chase her, beat on her van, curse her, and demand she take another driver's exam, but I didn't. I figured she was someone's grandmother, and I knew I wouldn't want someone to harass my grandmother just because she couldn't drive.

I didn't always know my grandmother could not drive. I only learned about her disability when I called my mother to see how my grandmother's eye doctor appointment had gone. Since my grandfather had died, her right knee had been replaced, and she was getting ready to have laser surgery on her eyes to remove cataracts. My mother answered on the third ring.

"Mom, I wanted to see how Granny's appointment went."

"The appointment went okay." She paused. "I guess."

"Did something happen? Is she okay?" I felt a thump in my chest.

"Well, you know how she is. You can't tell her a thing. She's gonna do what she wants."

I chuckled, knowing everything was all right; she had only made my mother mad about something, and I was curious to know more. "What'd she do?"

"Of course the doctor dilated her eyes, and she couldn't see a thing. When we got back to the house, she says, 'Well, I guess I better get going.' I said, 'Mama, you ain't going nowhere. You can't see a thing.' She told me, 'I can too see.' I figured if she could read the correct time on the clock above the fireplace, she'd be okay. 'What time does that clock say then?' She told me the right time, so I said, 'Okay, I reckon you'll be all right to drive then.' With that, she grabbed her purse, got in her car, and took off. I watched her drive away and knew when she couldn't keep that car in the sand ruts of the driveway that she was a disaster waiting to happen. Not three minutes later, I heard tires squealing and a crash that shook the ground. I couldn't bear to go see, so I sent your brother."

"Lord have mercy," I said. "Was she okay?"

"Oh yeah," Mom said. "She was fine. I guess. There was no sign of her, but an eighteen-wheeler lay on its side in the ditch. Your brother checked on the man and, aside from being mad as hell at the old lady who ran him off the road, he was fine. Of course, your brother didn't tell him it was Granny. The man said she just pulled right out in front of him. Didn't look or nothing. That ain't all. The highway men are painting the yellow lines in the center lanes on both sides of the highway and have these orange cones lined up for miles, so people won't mess up the paint. Your brother said she drove right down the center of the highway, knocking every cone out of her way for as far as he could see. Probably got that yellow paint all over her tires. Your brother said the Sheriff showed up, wrote a report, and put out an APB on her car. I'm too mad to call her. Mad at myself for letting her go and mad at her for being so damned stubborn."

When my mother said damn, I knew she was upset. Whenever she said it, she said it low while clenching her teeth.

I called my grandmother to check on her.

"I'm doing fine," she said.

"You have a little mishap today after your eye appointment?"

"I knew your Mama would tell everybody. Never could keep her mouth shut."

Of course, my Mother had told only me. She would have been too embarrassed to tell anyone else. My grandmother didn't say anything about the cones or the paint on her tires, and I didn't want to ask. When I asked why she didn't stop to check on the truck driver, she said, "Well, I figured if he was dead, I couldn't help him. If he was hurt, I couldn't do nothing either. If he was okay, he might beat me up."

I didn't tell my grandmother there was an all points bulletin for her vehicle. Quite frankly, I wanted to believe that would worry her. Truth is, I think she could have cared less because the sheriff is her cousin, and he wouldn't do a thing to her anyway. If he came to her house and tried, she'd fill him full of her blue ribbon pecan pie, and he'd forget all about it.

My grandmother had her cataracts removed and claims she can see as well as she used to when she was young. She was seventy-four, and now she is eighty and still driving, except when her new boyfriend takes her places. He's eighty-four.

My family first thought it was "cute" that my grandmother's hairdresser had matched her with an old widower even though she was scared to go out with him at first. "What if he takes me out on some back road and rapes me?" she had asked my mother.

"He's eighty-four. What could he possibly do?" Mom had responded.

When family called to check on her, she would be gone with him. Then family members said, "Better than sitting in front of the TV." After a few months, their attitudes changed. She didn't call them, and she was never home. When they did reach her, he was there, and she would cut them off, so they started saying, "Good God. A woman her age carrying on like a teenager. Daddy would turn over in his grave if he knew this."

I say go, Granny; the twilight years should be enjoyed.

Granny's Fight

When one generally thinks of his eighty-two-year-old grandmother, he doesn't generally think of the word fight, but my grandmother's fight riled our entire family. My grandmother's boyfriend, who was eighty-four, was dying of cancer and had been placed in a nursing home by his child Bertha, who was rumored to have slept with a pistol.

Bertha, afraid her Daddy might leave some of his money to my grandmother, had gone to court and tried to have the judge deem the old man incompetent to handle his affairs, so she could take control of his finances. The judge had ruled him competent to tend to his own affairs, and Bertha stormed from the courtroom, hysterically crying and carrying on to get sympathy.

Of course, none of that mattered, really. I called my grandmother, and the gentle soul I had always known her to be said, "I don't want that old man's money. I don't need it."

She didn't need it. She doesn't have a lot of money and mainly lives on social security, but need is a word her generation lived by. I, on the other hand, was more curious. "How much you reckon he's got?"

"Well," she said. "I imagine he's got a million in the bank

and another couple of million in timberland."

"My God," I said. What I wanted to tell my Grandmother was "Hell, if you don't think you need it, get it for the rest of us, who really don't need it either but wouldn't mind having it, for God's sake." I added, "You'd never know he had *any* money."

"No," she said. "You sure wouldn't. I reckon I'll go down to the nursing home tomorrow and check on him, but Bertha is mighty mad and I worry about that woman."

"You ain't got nothing to worry about," I said, trying to reassure her.

I received a call from my mother the next evening. She told me that my grandmother had gone to see her boyfriend only to find a "No Visitors, Except Family" sign on the door. She had inquired at the nurse's desk, and they told her she would not be permitted to see the old man. She left the nursing home extremely angry and upset. Her children, too, became upset, and one of my aunts called the judge. The judge didn't see any harm in two elderly people, who had spent so much time together, visiting and called the nursing home to inquire if the patient, or his doctor, had requested this. They had not. The perpetrator of the no visitor rule was Bertha. The judge told the nurses my grandmother could visit. My grandmother planned another visit the next day.

I called my mother the next evening to see how the second visit had gone. This time was actually worse for my grandmother. Upon entering the old man's room, Bertha became angry that my grandmother had won the visitors' battle and stormed out. In the process of storming out of the room to get security, or someone, anyone who would listen to her nagging, she shoved my grandmother who fell against the wall. Sore, but otherwise okay, my grandmother stayed a while and visited with her friend. I was happy it had all worked out, but I wanted to make the eight- hour drive and kick Bertha's big butt—along with every other relative who doesn't live there anymore.

The next day, Bertha regrouped and tried a different tactic to attempt to alleviate her fears. She called my mother and my mother's two sisters to convince them that my grandmother visiting her father was stressful for him and was causing him pain. A lot like their mother in their ability to be stubborn, the daughters did not give and refused to buy the sugarcoated argument from Bertha.

My grandmother visited her friend the third day, but one of my aunts accompanied her without incident. Next, Bertha used a different weapon of choice in her war. She contacted one of her father's former girlfriends to call my grandmother. My grandmother exchanged niceties with the woman.

"How you doing?" asked the old woman.

"Good, you?" responded my grandmother.

"Fine. I just wanted to check on Clem. I heard ya'll been seeing each other for a few months and thought you might know how he's doing."

"We've been seeing each other for about two years, but it's mighty nice of you to call. He's doing all right. Hanging in there," my grandmother said.

"Well, you know we dated for a couple of years up until sometime last year," the old woman said.

"I didn't know that," said my grandmother.

"Yeah, he used to call me his sugar baby," the old woman said.

My grandmother, who as I said earlier is a gentle soul and

rarely gets mad (or if she does, one wouldn't know it), said, "That's nice. Clem had asked me to marry him, but I said no. Did he ever ask you to marry him?"

"No, he didn't. Well, I need to go, but it's been good talking to you." The old woman hung up the phone.

The rest of the afternoon my grandmother spent time on the phone telling family members about how her dying friend had been not only two-timing her with some other old woman, but also had called that old woman his sugar baby, too, and how she didn't care if he was dying or not, but that she wasn't going to be treated like that by any man and how she was gonna go down to that nursing home and give him a piece of her mind. I didn't want to call her. Figured she'd just get upset all over again having to tell me the story.

Whether she told him off or not, I do not know. My guess is that she came up with some way of letting him know how she felt without upsetting him. Clem didn't last much longer, but they continued to visit till the day before he died, when he slipped into a coma. My grandmother did not attend his funeral because she was sick and because she did not want to face Bertha, who would be hysterically crying, but also glad to finally have the money. In fact, within a month, Bertha had a new house in a prestigious subdivision and had sold all the timberland.

My grandmother quietly grieved and now fights cancer— a harder battle for her. The cancer would have been caught sooner if she had kept her appointment instead of canceling to check on Clem.

Honeymoon

The marriage ceremony itself wasn't all that bad, but getting to the ceremony was a hellish experience. My fiancée and her bridesmaids had left early to be pampered at the Ritz-Carlton in Naples, Florida, which is where we had finally decided to have the immediate-family-only wedding after some grueling months of planning. When my soon-to-be father-in-law learned the costs associated with having the hometown wedding, due to the six hundred guests, he made a proposition: "Ya'll go off somewhere, have a nice, small wedding with some of the family, and I'll give you the difference in cash to put toward your bills," he said.

"That sounds great," I said, running through my list of bills.

My fiancée Julia, on the other hand, had tears in her eyes. "I wanted a big wedding," she whined.

"This will be better," I reassured. "Those people just want to come and get a free meal. They don't give a damn about us getting married. In fact, if we get gifts, they'll be cheap crap we'll have to re-gift or throw away."

We ended up having more of the same conversation later, but eventually, she came around and decided The Ritz would

51

be elegant, cool, and different. I asked for one thing: a bag-pipe player. I loved bagpipe music and actually wanted to learn how to play them, but I found out they were expensive and, after many years of smoking, I probably didn't have the lung capacity to play them anyway.

The night before I drove the eight-hour trip to Naples, I spent the night with my friends, Jacob and Janine. Both had backgrounds as counselors, and I think they befriended me in graduate school thinking they could help me. I had asked Jacob to be in the wedding, so he and Janine followed me in their Miata to Naples. I drove Julia's Eclipse, and somewhere along the boring interstate, I noticed their lights flashing. I pulled off and Jacob told me the Eclipse was polluting. We noticed the origin of the smoke was from under the hood. I managed to make it to Lake City, where I pulled into a ga-rage. After I excitedly explained my dilemma about getting married the next day and needing to be there for the rehearsal dinner a few hours away, they agreed to check the car as best and as quickly as they could. What I learned was that upon having the oil changed before I left the dealership in Georgia, the mechanic failed to put the oil plug back in, thereby causing all of the oil to leak out onto the motor. It was a miracle the car didn't catch on fire or that the engine did not lock. Hours later, we were back on the interstate heading toward Naples.

I don't recall much about Naples, except the Ritz, since that's the only place I went. Situated on the Gulf of Mexico, the stately Ritz seemed a horseshoe. The brick courtyard overlooked the white sandy beaches and crystal clear sea. The wedding took place the next morning, and even though Au-gust temperatures by noon were near a hundred degrees, the sea breeze kept us cool. Five minutes before the wedding, the bagpipe player had yet to materialize, so the Ritz employees hauled a baby grand piano to the courtyard and had an employee play the music. (For their mistake, I received a free night's stay at any Ritz in the world, which alleviated my anger at the moment even though I could not afford to go anywhere in the world.) As I stood with the minister, our wedding party flanking us, our families seated, and "The Bridal Chorus" being hammered on the piano, Julia was escorted by her father through the courtyard. I don't recall much about the ceremony, except the vows: for richer or poorer. I remember chuckling at that one when I repeated it. After the "I do's" and the infamous kiss, we walked back toward the Ritz and were applauded by guests and employees standing on room balconies. The clapping sounds echoing through the courtyard caught us by surprise, and we waved and felt like a king and queen.

After we had brunch, made pictures, and changed clothes, we left for our honeymoon, which I had proudly planned. We were to spend a night in a resort on an island just off the coast. There were no bridges, so I had chartered a boat. I didn't realize when booking the boat that the "captain," as he referred to himself when he happily took my credit card number over the phone, was actually going to chauffeur us to the island in a metal, two-seater fishing boat.

Prior to boarding the "charter" boat, the captain advised us to buy mosquito repellant in the bait and tackle store. I did, even though I couldn't believe the small bottle cost nearly ten dollars. Aboard the vessel, the captain did redeem himself somewhat by touring us through groves and pointing out some of the history associated with the area. Unfortunately, just as he was expounding on the history of the island we were destined for, a flock of gulls flew over and dumped their waste into the water, the boat, and onto Julia's going away dress and sun bonnet. After the shock settled, and the twice divorced, half-drunk captain said, "That's what marriage is like," we laughed it off.

We exited the boat as it rocked in the shallows of the marina and once again, I reminded the captain what time to pick us up the next day. Of course, since I had paid in advance for the trip, I was worried that he would not return. The motel, once home to a famous writer whom I do not recall ever having heard about, appeared more run-down and dirty than the pictures and article of the quaint getaway (on the Native American built shell mound) *Southern Living* had described.

I was most disappointed when we entered our room. Just off the hallway next to the kitchen, our honeymoon suite's wooden door barely closed, the quaint crystal doorknob was for looks and did not turn, and the rusted latch seemed as though it would come out of the wood with the least amount of pressure. The sheets looked clean, but the spider webs in the windows and on the ceiling had captured several bugs, which I thought was a cost effective way of having a building exterminated; the ceramic tub, however, had a few roaches crawling about. I turned on the water to wash them down the drain, and the dark water left grains of black dirt and rust in the tub.

Julia and I changed clothes and went for a walk about the island. We climbed the water tower, which was also a viewing tower, only to be attacked by hundreds of mosquitoes. The ten-dollar spray had apparently worn off. We scratched our way down the tower and into the restaurant for an early dinner and swallowed the food I feared had been cooked with the same water from our tub. We did, however, drink bottled soda.

Needless to say, our honeymoon was not the romantic evening we had imagined. Fortunately, we had Benadryl to help with the itching, and our exhausted bodies fell asleep to the sounds of pots and pans banging in the kitchen and the ceiling fan's jerking. The next morning, we awoke to the heat and humidity that no jerking ceiling fan, caked with dust, could alleviate. We had dreamed of air conditioning and prayed our captain would come early to return us to the mainland. Prayers answered, we returned safely and quickly drove north on the interstate to a cooler climate with a lack of mosquitoes.

Somewhere near Atlanta, I told Julia: "I didn't have bagpipes at my wedding, but would you see to it they play at my funeral?"

"Sure," she said.

I guessed it wouldn't matter to me much if bagpipes played or not, but it would probably annoy everyone else who attended.

Luck

After we moved into our house, I decided to do some yard work and clipped my finger, instead of the boxwood, with the pruning shears; I scrambled into the house in search of a Band-Aid. My wife Julia would have known if there were any Band-Aids in the house, but she was spending my money getting her nails done at a salon. Quite frankly, I was glad she was out of my way because she had been flitting about the house, singing, and she couldn't carry a tune. I didn't know why she was so happy, but I resented it.

The white carpet with blood spots looked like chicken pox and reminded me of Lily Tomlin on "Laugh-In" when she connected the dots. I wrapped my finger with half a roll of paper towels, knowing that if I had bought the quicker picker upper instead of the cheap brand I would not need so many. I noticed the mailman's jeep at the mailbox and walked out the front door and down the sidewalk, cursing the pruning shears that still lay by the boxwood. I gathered the bundle of junk, but was intrigued by a letter from a doctor. I opened it first because as an attention-getter to get newcomers' business, he had stapled a Band-Aid at the top.

I promptly used the Band-Aid and thought for the first

time in twenty-five years that my luck might be changing. I had always identified myself with the guys in coveralls on "Hee-Haw" who moaned, "If it weren't for bad luck, I'd have no luck at all," because of marijuana and losing the Florida lottery.

* * * *

When I was single and in college at a university in Georgia, I discovered that one drawback to being white and middle-class was that I was unable to get federal grant money for college, because my parents made too much money, although I never knew it. I had to work full time to pay tuition and living expenses. When I left campus for the three o'clock to eleven o'clock shift at the Ramada in my 1978 Buick Regal, I was embarrassed because the silver paint flaked, and the tailpipe left clouds of choking smoke behind. I had bought the car because the electric windows and gray velvet seats made me feel like I was moving up in the world, and though it was already ten years old and needed major engine work, it was as comfortable as a coffin, except for the lack of air conditioning. In the middle of dog days in South Georgia, no air conditioning can be a death sentence, but I was able to take extended cold showers in the dorm, which kept me from pouring sweat on the way to work.

Before the electric door opened at the motel, I caught a glimpse of myself in the glass: Hushpuppy loafers, Duckhead khakis, and a plaid shirt. I looked more like a golfer than a motel clerk. I dreaded talking to Sam, the day clerk and assistant manager who had formerly been a minister till he got caught with his hand in the Baptist church's cookie jar and in his secretary's blouse. He loved giving unsolicited advice.

"How're you?" Sam plopped on the counter, his imitation

gold Rolex glittering under the recessed lighting above the maroon counter.

"Pretty good," I said. "Sure is hot out there." I had learned early on in life the weather can be a great topic of discussion when you want to avoid talking.

"You know what?" he asked.

That was his favorite question because he knew any polite Southerner would respond, giving him the ammunition to ramble. "What?"

"It's never been this hot before," Sam said. "I honestly believe it's getting worse. It's in Revelation. All this evil in the world is rotting us away. One day, there won't be nothing left." Sam's eyes rolled in their sockets, focusing beyond the windows. I knew he had spaced out because there was nothing to look at, except the dumpster behind the Sewanee Swifty; I also knew that the evil he enjoyed talking about so much was within himself.

"You're probably right." I knew the best way to reach success was to agree with others even when you didn't. You never know when you might need a reference.

"I'm convinced that the root to it all is drugs. It's just so easy to get hooked, and they can destroy a person." Sam's hands trembled. I had often smelled alcohol on his breath when I came to work, and I figured he probably had a drinking problem. I also knew he could only help himself.

"Lot of drugs out there," I said, taking the cash drawer out and counting the money. Although it wasn't required that employees check the money when changing shifts, I had been told by the manager, a former Baptist follower, to check Sam's drawer every time. I did. Lord knows I couldn't have paid a shortage, which was the company's illegal policy.

"You ever do drugs?" Sam's eyes were piercing, and I felt my face flush.

"No," I said and nervously laughed. It wasn't that I had done drugs and was lying, but I had been offered drugs at fraternity parties, and I had seriously considered it. No matter how innocent I was, I always felt guilty in the presence of one who claimed to know God better than me since I was too busy studying, working, and socializing. "But I did find a field of marijuana once."

"Whose was it?"

I wondered why he wanted to know. "That's the funny part," I said. "It didn't belong to nobody."

"What do you mean?" Sam grimaced, and I knew he didn't want to hear me talk.

"Well, me and Felton, my friend from childhood, went through this cornfield to fish in the woods, and we discovered all this marijuana. We ran home and called the police. We were told we'd get a reward, so we went to the hardware store and got new bikes. The police sent the marijuana off to the GBI lab in Atlanta, and about a week later, the chief came to tell us the marijuana wasn't marijuana. It was some wild weed that looks just like marijuana. Our parents made us return the bikes since we weren't going to get any reward money."

Sam chuckled, and his belly shimmied. "I better get on out of here. Money check out?"

"Yeah, perfect."

Sam nodded and gathered his newspaper. "Give me a call if you need anything."

I knew it would be a slow night because we didn't have many reservations: a regular Frito-Lay trucker, shampoo salesman, and three unknowns. The unknowns were booked by the central reservation system, and I could bet money they were either Yankees or Canadians on their way to Disney World. I could also bet money they would ask me to repeat myself, delighting in the cuteness of my Southern drawl and reinforcing their notion that Southerners are stupid. It was them, however, that had been suckered off the interstate and would pay prices too high for everything. My grandmother had been right in the sense that the South would rise again, at least in their ability to take Northerners' money for choles-terol-laced food, uncomfortable beds in cockroach-infested rooms, and tourist attractions like mosquito-breeding alligator farms or chigger-infested moss gardens.

I tuned the lobby TV to CNN and hoped I didn't need to call Sam since he never answered his phone and didn't have an answering machine. Sam did usually call back shortly after I would call, though, just to check on things. The evening passed slowly, and I found myself being amused by bugs hov-ering around the outside lights and the repetitive headlines. My eyes grew heavy, and each time a car pulled under the awning, my body, like a robot, managed to find the energy to lift itself up and check the weary traveler in only to shuffle back to its position in front of headline news. At nine o'clock, I got up, locked the door, and opened the venetian blinds cov-ering the night check-in window. Though some desk clerks opted not to use the half-moon window, I did for fear of being robbed. I positioned myself in the desk chair, listened to the hum of the portable fan, and closed my eyes.

In the dream, a man dressed in a business suit stood at the counter and said, "3-2-2." The numbers echoed about the lobby, and I kept asking him what he meant. And he repeated them over and over, and they continued to echo. When I was pulled awake by a banging noise, I jumped up and sprinted to the glass door to unlock it for the graveyard clerk, Bill. He looked half asleep, and although I didn't know him well at all, I had heard he worked the audit shift because he got nervous around people.

"You been sleeping?" He poured day-old coffee into a styrofoam cup.

"No, just resting my eyes." A lie and the response I learned from my dad.

"Anything happening?" He began straightening folios in the tray and seemed bothered by the ones that were not perfectly aligned with the metal separators; then, Bill moved to the circular phone stand where last names and room numbers were alphabetized. He straightened those, too.

"Quiet night," I said. "You gonna count the money?"

"No," Bill said. "You can go on."

"Thanks." I headed out the door, looking back at Bill who was straightening the pen attached to the desk by a chain rope. He lifted the pen into the air and made the chains form a circular pattern like the lines on a conch shell.

I felt most people were screwed up in one way or another, and I looked forward to the day I was out of college with a real job, making lots of money. I sank into the velvet seats, cranked the Regal, and watched the smoke roll out and upward into the lights, confusing the bugs. I pressed the button and the window came down, and I breathed in the humid night air. As I drove down the street, I thought about the dream and the man's echoing numbers. On one level, I knew the dream was important and intuitively felt the numbers were the key to the Florida lottery, which was up to sixty million.

I was off the next day, and after class, I sat in my room, scribbling 322 onto a note pad and thinking about my new BMW, beach house, and all the European trips I would take. I told my roommate, David, "You watch. These numbers are my ticket out of here." He smirked and replied, "All that partying your freshman year has had an effect on you." I knew David would be jealous when I won, and I drove the twenty miles down Interstate 75 to the Florida line and spent my last twenty dollars on tickets. I picked various numbers and included combinations from my dream numbers. That night, I couldn't sleep. I knew I did not have the right number combination. So, when I got paid on Friday, I cashed my check, and instead of making my car payment, I drove back to the Florida line, stood in line for two hours, and spent my entire week's pay on more tickets. I told others in line: "You're wasting your time; I've got the numbers." They politely smiled, but I could see fear in their eyes.

When ten o'clock came on Saturday night, I used the courtesy phone in the lobby to call my parents to tell them I was going to win the lottery. "That's nice," my mother said. "Don't forget about us." I knew she didn't believe me, and when she asked, "Are you okay?" I knew she thought I was crazy. When eleven o'clock finally came, Bill was obsessively straightening, and I plopped down onto the sofa in front of the TV. I watched the painted ping-pong balls float upward in the plastic bubbles. My heart raced, and even though the air conditioning was on in the lobby, beads of sweat rolled down my sides from my armpits. As the carnival music played, and the blonde lottery woman with breasts bursting at the seams of her blue sequined dress said the numbers into the camera, my heart sank. Though I had over one hundred and fifty tickets, I knew the winning numbers were not on my tickets. Still, I wrote them down and reassured myself.

I stayed up till two in the morning, checking and rechecking my tickets and wondering how I would ever make my car payment. Sunday morning, I ate breakfast in the university cafe and read in the paper that a homeless woman in Tampa, living in her station wagon with three children, spent her last dollar on a lottery ticket and won. I laughed and rationalized she needed it more than I did. The BMW became a Regal, the beach house became my dorm room, and the European trips became trips to the Ramada.

* * * *

When Julia came back from the beauty salon, I told her about cutting my finger, finding the Band-Aid in the doctor's marketing letter, and how I believed my luck might be changing.

"Sit down," she said, smiling.

I sat in the green wicker chair. "What is it? Did you win some money?"

"No," she said and laughed. "I'm pregnant. I didn't want to tell you first thing this morning because you were so busy in the yard."

I had the same sinking feeling I had the time I found out the marijuana wasn't real and the time I didn't win the lottery. "Sure is hot in here," I said, wiping my forehead. I stayed in a feverish state for weeks till Julia told me, "False alarm."

Newlyweds

Our first year of marriage, Julia and I had a lot to learn about each other. Normally I would buy a case of grapefruit when I'd visit family in South Georgia because it's cheaper, but when I saw the flier in the newspaper advertising grapefruit ten for a dollar at a local grocery store, I decided to splurge and buy enough to last us awhile. Julia said she'd juice them in our juicer, a wedding gift that had collected dust in the closet with so many others. When Julia and I arrived at the store, we grabbed a cart and began filling, making sure the soft, indented grapefruits were put back. Finished, we decided to pick up a few more items we needed, so we pushed our cart full of grapefruit around till we had everything. Some people stared and I speculated they could sense my pleasure at getting a bargain.

The lines weren't that long, and when we finally reached the cashier, she seemed pleasant enough.

"How're ya'll doing?" She stared at the items in the cart and began grabbing everything, except the grapefruit.

"Pretty good," I mumbled, handing her my grocery store discount card.

She scanned the card first, passed it back to me, and ran

the items across so fast that I could barely keep up with the prices flashing on the cash register screen. My wife watched me and sensed my nervousness. She thought it both amazing and annoying, as she had told me, that I could memorize every price of every item I put in the buggy, which enabled me to check the scanner to make sure I wasn't getting ripped off. Sure enough, the scanner was wrong practically every time we had gone to the grocery store, and most cashiers tried to avoid me. Their plastic lights would flicker off when they saw me approach, and they would suddenly disappear on break. But this cashier who scanned these items was new.

When she scanned the first grapefruit, the screen showed twenty-five cents. I could feel the frustration. "That's not right," I said. "The grapefruits are ten for a dollar."

"Well, it'll probably take the discount off at the end."

"Oh, okay," I said.

"How many of these do you have?"

"Sixty."

She smirked. "You must like grapefruit."

When the total appeared, I knew it was wrong. "The computer didn't take the discount."

"Then they must be twenty-five cents," she said.

"No, the flier said ten cents. So did the sign."

One aisle over, a redheaded cashier, who had never been friendly, said, "They're a quarter apiece." She smiled at her customer and mumbled, "Just can't please some of them."

Enraged, I raised my voice and pointed. "You mind your business over there."

The redhead's face suddenly matched her hair. My cashier turned red, too, and the lady behind me with three kids in tow began scanning aisles and backing up.

"You get the manager over here," I demanded.

She flipped the switch on the microphone. "Manager to four."

After what seemed like twenty minutes, the pear-shaped manager rocked his way to the cash register. "He says the grapefruit is ten for a dollar," the cashier said to the manager.

"They're a quarter apiece," he said. The redhead, still not minding her business, turned and smiled.

"The flier said ten for a dollar. The sign said ten for a dollar. I can't believe ya'll don't even know what is on sale," I barked.

"I don't believe they *are* on sale," pear man said.

Julia had moved back to the magazine rack and was flipping pages. I knew she didn't want them to think she was with me. "Let's go," I said, signaling to the cashier and pear man and snapping my fingers (another trait my wife hated). "You, too," I added to the redhead.

They followed me to fruits and vegetables, where I pointed to the sign. "Do you all see that sign?"

The manager turned to my cashier and said, "Ten for a dollar." He waddled toward baked goods, and the redhead sprinted back to her register. The cashier nodded at the bagger, giving him the go ahead to bag the grapefruit. I guess he had not wanted to bag them if I didn't buy them. The cashier made the correction, and I paid. I found Julia outside staring at the half-dead mums. "What are you doing?" I asked

"Well, I thought we could get some of these."

"You're kidding, right?"

"No," she said.

"They're half dead. If I get you some, it'll be after they close, and I won't pay a dime for them."

"You're so damned tight," she snapped.

I chuckled. I had heard it before from friends, family, and even from people I met who had heard it from someone else. Every time I found a deal, I had a habit of telling everyone I knew about it. When I found a pair of Cole-Haan shoes at the dead man shoe store for ten dollars, I spent over a hundred dollars in long distance calls telling people about it, which doesn't make sense. Since that deal, I had not bought a pair of new shoes in seven years; I got them all at the dead man shoe store. Actually, the store didn't sell shoes they got from dead people; they were used shoes. I had taken my family and Julia's family there to hunt for bargains. My father-in-law had bought a pair of shoes there, believing they had come from a dead man since I had never told him any different. He slipped on wet steps at his house and nearly broke his back. The next time I talked with Milton on the phone, he said, "You're right. Those are dead man shoes. They nearly killed me, too." But Milton wouldn't think about passing up a deal.

Julia was still angry, or acted that way, on the drive home. Mostly, I suppose she was embarrassed, but I felt she should be used to my tightness, my creative penny pinching or frugalness, as I preferred to call it. It was a behavior I learned first from my childhood Sunday school teacher-employer and one that was reinforced by my father.

Trying to soothe, I told Julia about Miss Emma, a housewife and all-around active member of the community, especially in church where she taught my Sunday school class. I worked for Miss Emma and Mr. Virgil, the town banker, in the 1970s when I was twelve after I decided I wanted to earn my own money instead of waiting for an allowance, and I accepted their offer to do gardening for a dollar an hour.

Miss Emma had small, dark tadpole eyes, sandy brown hair, which was teased and sprayed stiff, and a jabbing elbow that she used when I was out of line in Sunday school, poking me in the rib cage till I stopped snickering. Miss Emma always wore dresses, hose, and pumps, and once I was employed, she led me around the manicured yard, pointing out her azalea gardens lined with monkey grass. On the right side of the back yard were cement stepping stones leading to a blue looking glass ball resting atop of a cement pedestal. She told me Mister Virgil had ordered it for her from Chicago. I asked her what it was for, and she said to keep the bugs out of her garden. I wondered how the blue ball could do that, and Miss Emma said they saw their ugly reflection and flew off.

So I edged the driveway, mowed the carpet-like grass, and pulled weeds all through the humid summer, drinking gifts of bottled Coke and eating slices of homemade prune cake, till the leaves began to change. Miss Emma told me she would call when it was time to rake. When she did, I showed up, and she gave me a cane fishing pole instead of a rake. She instructed me to climb the maple trees and beat the leaves out. Bewildered, I did as instructed for fear of her elbow. After the tree was bare, I climbed down, raked, and burned the leaves in a rusted oil barrel behind the property.

Miss Emma paid me for the day and said maybe next spring if I was not busy, I could come back to work. She did not need me any more since there were no other leaf-bearing trees in her yard—just long leaf pines, which dropped straw she used for mulch.

"That's a great story about being cheap," Julia said. "But you act ugly to people when you think you're right."

"No," I corrected. "I only get ugly when I know I'm right

and others won't admit it. There's a difference."

"Well, I don't think you get your cheapness from Miss Emma. Do you think you get it from your Dad?"

"Actually," I said, "I get it from Mom and Dad. They're both bargain shoppers, and I guess if you've got four kids, you have to be that way."

"Yeah, that's true. But they're not the same."

"No, they're not. Dad is more laid back, and Mom's got the temper. I get that from her. I wouldn't change it either. You get more done that way. Dad, though, goes beyond looking for bargains and discounts. He tries to get stuff free."

"What do you mean?" she quizzed.

I explained to Julia that since we were newlyweds, and she had not spent a Christmas with my family, she did not know about Dad's stocking-stuffer gifts yet. Each year, Dad would go to businesses all over town and get free calendars, pens, pencils, grippers, note pads—basically anything a business was giving away—and stuff the items in our stockings. My brothers and sister would get a kick out of the freebies, but they usually came in handy during the year and probably saved us a little money. "It goes way beyond the stocking stuffers, though. The pizza pans, for example."

"Pizza pans?"

"Yep. Didn't you notice that pizza pan we got for a wedding gift?"

"Yeah. I thought that was a great idea. Did that come from your Dad?" she asked.

"Sure did. What did you do with it?"

"I guess I put it in the cabinet."

"Did you notice it was used?"

"What?"

69

"You heard me. Used. Years ago, he got some used deep dish pizza pans from a pizza restaurant and started wrapping them up with a dollar pizza cutter and a box of pizza mix and giving them away as wedding gifts."

"You've got to be kidding," Julia said.

"Nope. People said it was the most unique gift they got."

"What did your Mom say?"

"What could she say? If they've got anything at all in common, it's their determination. So I inherited a double dose of that."

"Great," she said.

We pulled into the driveway and unloaded the grapefruit and other items. I told Julia I would cook a pizza for supper after I took a nap—the incident in the grocery store had worn me out. I heard the juicer going and beeps from the phone being dialed. I knew Julia was calling Rebecca, her best friend to whom she would tell all this latest news. Part of me wondered if she would've gone through with the wedding if she had known about the familial quirks before the ceremony. I was glad I had not told her all of them.

Not Harper Lee

Before we drifted off to sleep, the rain was lightly falling—enough to be soothing like a children's song from *Sesame Street*. We awoke to rain pelting the roof and windows, thunder booming, and the duct vents on the roof spinning round and round like tops from the high winds. I was already awake, waiting for Julia to become conscious and tell me to go get our dog and bring her in. She would demand I get the dog out of fear that the dog would be struck by lightning. Her father had been struck, so naturally, she would think that. Although her father had not been seriously injured and suffered no long-term effects, he did make more money afterwards. I secretly wished I could be hit by lightning, if more money would be the result.

Julia flung off the covers. "Go check on Harper Lee!" she yelled. My only contribution to "her baby" was its name: the author Harper Lee had not responded to my request for an interview, and so I felt the name quite fitting.

"It's storming, dammit," I said, clearing my throat. "She's an outside dog, and she'll be all right."

"Come on," she whimpered. "She might get hit by lightning."

I knew if I did not get out of bed, Julia would. "The storm

will pass," I said.

A flash of lightning and her tone changed. "Well," she snapped, "If you won't, I will." She sprang out of bed and threw on her plaid robe.

"No," I conceded. "I'll go get her." I was going to risk my life for a dog. But, I rationalized, I did want to smoke.

I stumbled onto the dark porch, flicking the light. The wind was blowing too much, and I cupped my hand to get a flame. As I deeply inhaled the smoke, Harper Lee jumped on the porch. "Damn," I said, "how'd you get off your chain?" Although perplexed by the dog's ability to get loose, I was relieved I wouldn't have to venture into the storm. I petted her wet head and immediately wanted to wash my hands. Hearing me talking to Harper Lee, Julia opened the storm door, and the dog rushed in.

"This is not Harper Lee!" she screamed.

A big black dog that looked part Rottweiler and part Chow was running around the living room, happy to be inside. But he looked mean, and I did not want to go in. "Help me get him out of here," she said, moving toward him. I opened the storm door and tiptoed inside. Julia grabbed his collar. The black dog growled, showing white fangs and a blue tongue, and I thought of the *Omen* movies.

I stayed in place by the door. "I'll hold the door, and you pull him out." She didn't need to know I was scared to death; after all, that would only increase her fear.

Although the stubborn black dog dug in like a soldier, Julia managed to show him onto the porch and slam the wooden door shut, leaving me on the porch, still holding the storm door open, with the evil dog. "Good boy," I stuttered, not hearing my words for the pounding heartbeat, which had moved into my throat and head. When I closed the storm door, he growled again, and then curled in a ball, guarding the door and blocking my entrance.

I lit another cigarette, wondering how I would get inside.

Julia peered through the window. "Is he gone?"

"Hell no," I barked. "How am I supposed to get inside?"

"I don't know," she said. "What about Harper Lee?"

"To hell with Harper Lee!" I yelled.

The storm briefly subsided, so I decided to walk off the porch and down the driveway to the road to see if the dog would follow. He did. When I turned to run back to the house, the black dog did so, too, growling at my heels. Back on the porch, I began sneezing, knowing that if I survived the night, I'd catch a cold. I wondered if Harper Lee was worth all the trouble.

After taking its interlude, the storm returned even more fiercely. "We're under a tornado warning," Julia yelled through the window.

"Great." I made up my mind that Harper Lee was a goner. She had chewed up every toy I bought for her, she refused to accept the behavioral conditioning I'd learned from Skinnerian psychology, and she had cost me a fortune in veterinarian bills. The only positive thing was that Harper Lee had won the Jack Daniel's country dog contest at the yearly international barbecue. For that, she had received a bag of bones, twenty-five dollars, and a trophy. The money did not begin to reimburse me for my expenses. Now, however, what concerned me was that I had been forced out of my own house.

With the storm back in full force, the evil dog would not leave the porch. I hatched a plan to get myself back inside. "Go unlock the back door, and I'll sneak around," I ordered Julia through the window. She nodded.

I darted off the porch, and when I reached the side of the

house, I peeked back around the corner. The evil dog was still there, guarding the front door. So far so good. I ran to the back door and turned the knob. It was locked. I stood in the torrent, getting drenched. At least the front of the house had a covered porch. I pounded on the door. Finally, Julia ambled to the door and unlocked it, and I rushed in. "Where the hell were you?"

"I'm sorry," she said. "I forgot."

"Forgot?" Someone forgets to turn off the coffee pot or to turn off a light. Someone does not forget to let her husband in before he gets killed in a storm or eaten by Cujo. I stomped through the house to the front door to see if the evil dog was still on the porch. He was.

When the evil dog saw that I was safely inside, he stood on his hind legs, looking through the window and barking repeatedly at me. "You kiss my ass," I told him.

"That dog doesn't understand you," Julia said.

"Oh yeah he does," I assured. The storm began to ease.

"Well?" she said, cocking her head. "Are you gonna go get Harper Lee?"

"To hell with Harper Lee," I repeated. "I'm going to bed." Julia didn't argue. I guess the storm's subsiding made her feel better about the safety of her baby. My soggy body collapsed onto the bed, and I fell fast asleep. The next day, the black dog was gone, and I tried to forget about him, although I did worry about some of my elderly neighbors having a similar encounter and having a stroke or heart attack.

About three weeks later, I was driving through town; there was the black dog, slinking down the sidewalk. I blew the horn. I glanced in the rear view mirror and saw him barking.

Plastic Jesus

Regardless of whether the myth of the full moon causing people to act stranger than usual is true, admissions at the mental hospital were on the rise, and as an admissions counselor, I had been asked to work overtime. I felt my title was ironic. Sure, I admitted patients, but counseling consisted of following a list of questions on a standard form. Coffee filled me with a false sense of energy, masking my burnout and inauthenticity. Often, I had thought of quitting my job, but more often than not, the monetary reward every two weeks (even with uncle Sam's rather large cut) kept me employed— that is till the night of the full moon when I worked with two patients who pushed me past the edge. Even coffee could not jump-start me.

I unlocked the glass door for the two deputies who had brought in a regular patient. Calling him a regular makes him sound more like a customer in a motel than a mental patient, but he was hauled in at least once a month after not taking his medication for schizophrenia. Interestingly enough, life experiences for him seemed more fantastic when not on the medication, even though experiences for others became sur-realistic nightmares. I nicknamed him Goliath because of his size and violent tendencies.

"How are you doing?" I stood in the doorway as the deputies walked him inside. He was wearing cuffs on his ankles and hands. He didn't respond, which was no surprise to me. What was surprising, however, was when the deputies unlocked the cuffs, told me to have a nice evening, and started out the door.

"Can't you guys stay till I get him admitted?" I whispered. I worked alone in admissions on the night shift, and though I had back-up from technicians on the units, it took them several minutes to make it through all the locked doors. I could be dead by the time they arrived with restraints.

"We're extremely busy tonight," one deputy said. "It is a full moon, you know."

"Yes," I said, locking the door as they left.

I turned to Goliath, who was nodding to one of the chairs in the waiting room. I knew he was hallucinating. "I'll be right back. Do you want something to drink?"

No response. I walked to my office, found his file, and quickly reviewed it before returning to the lobby. On his last visit, I had admitted him and made notes about his behavior. An imaginary dog had accompanied him, and Goliath wouldn't speak. He had only barked. Though I had not written this in the chart, I had barked back to see if he would respond. He had by asking me if I was crazy, too.

Whether from coffee or fear, my heart fluttered, and I took a seat across from Goliath, the metal chart in my lap. Still, no eye contact. "You feeling okay?"

Goliath nodded, his eyes squinting at me. I didn't know if he was attempting to see into this world, or if he was seeing something else instead of me. Still squinting, he said, "Demons is everywhere."

"Yes, they are," I said, looking around and focusing on the Monet print.

"You a demon?"

"No," I said.

Goliath did not respond but stared at my eyes, which made me even more nervous.

"May I ask you some questions?"

He nodded.

I asked him if he knew the date, time, and who the President of the United States was. While I waited for him to respond, I figured if I ever had to answer these questions, I might be considered not fully oriented, too. I rarely could remember the date and didn't know the time unless I checked my watch. The President was easy, since he was always in the news for some scandal or another.

"Lincoln," he slurred.

"Okay," I said, making a note. Well, at least he answered something.

"You been getting enough rest?"

"Nah," he said, turning his attention to the Monet. I guess my boss had been right about the Monet. When they refurbished the lobby, I had asked that they select a Van Gogh to hang, but they felt his work might agitate; Monet was more soothing.

Realizing this could go on all night, I decided to call the unit and ask the techs to come get Goliath. One of the cardinal rules during my training had been to make no sudden moves, but the coffee had made me hyper, and I jumped up. Before I realized what was going on, Goliath was in my face, the switchblade at my throat.

"It's okay," I whispered. "I'm sorry if I startled you. I'm just going to get you something to help you relax."

"You's a demon. I could see it around you."

I didn't like bringing religion into this. "I believe in God, and God tells me he loves you."

Goliath backed away a few inches, but the blade still pointed at me.

"God tells me he wants me to help you, so I would like to go and get you something to help you relax, okay?" I would have been put on notice had my boss known I said such things, but I felt whatever worked was all right.

Goliath moved further away. "Okay," he said, sitting in the chair and resting the blade on his knee.

I tiptoed toward my office, where I closed the door and locked it. I called the unit, told them he had a knife, but was calm. I sat wiping the sweat beads from my brows and sipping more coffee, though I didn't need the caffeine with the adrenaline pumping in my system. When I heard the doors being unlocked, I crept out of my office and met the techs and nurse in the hall. "He'll be okay," I assured, and he was. He gave up the knife and went calmly to the unit. I wondered why the deputies had not frisked him, but chalked it up to the moon.

It was three in the morning before the buzzer on the door rang again. I sprinted to the door to see an older woman and young girl.

"Come on in," I said. "Have a seat over there." Both looked normal, so I wasn't sure who I would be dealing with. Once I retrieved a new form and my metal clipboard, I returned and took a seat across from them. Both were well dressed, looked groomed, and the old woman was holding the young girl's hand. "How may I help you?"

"This is Felicia, my granddaughter," the old woman said. "She's been having some problems."

"What sort of problems?"

"She's not sleeping and she's seeing things."

"What sort of things is she seeing?"

"People who ain't there. The world turning to liquid."

"How old is she?"

"Seventeen."

"Ever had any problems before?"

"Aside from colds, no. We go to church. She's a straight A student. Plays sports. She's popular and got a good boy-friend. I don't know what's happening." The grandmother dabbed a handkerchief at the corner of her eyes.

"How long has this been going on?"

"About three weeks," she said.

"Any problems in the family?"

"Not my side. Don't know her daddy, and her mama run off when she was a baby. I raised her myself."

"Is she taking any drugs?" I hated to ask, but I had to.

"No," her grandmother scolded.

It did not take a lot to see the girl was having some prob-lems. She scanned the walls, raising her eyebrows, smiling or frowning, and occasionally mumbling. I knew she was halluci-nating, and while most patients I had seen were products of a revolving door system, this young lady did not fit the mold. I did feel sorry for her, for her grandmother. I assumed that her brain chemistry was out of whack, and I hated the thought she would have to take medication for the rest of her life— medi-cation science didn't know the long term effects of. I hated that she might be labeled by a society that did not care, that she would have to be admitted to a place like this because she had no insurance and could not afford better care. Most of all, I hated that I could do nothing, that my education and training seemed useless.

"Felicia, I'm here to help you. Do you want me to help you?" When the words left my mouth, I knew how empty they were, but I was so used to saying them.

Her eyes turned toward me, and she nodded. "I know who you are."

"You do?" I thought she recognized me from the grocery store or a restaurant.

"You're Jesus." She smiled.

I looked at her grandmother who just shook her head back and forth. I could not count the times I had been called a demon. Earlier that night, I had been called a demon, but I had never been called Jesus.

"Felicia, I'm not Jesus," I said in my most soothing voice. "I'm a counselor here at the hospital." I pointed to my name-tag pinned to my white coat.

"Why would you lie to me, Jesus?"

I scooted to the edge of my seat and extended my arm. "Touch my hand. See, I'm not Jesus." I wanted to get through to her. I felt it could be the moment of truth—that if she could see I was not the supernatural being she thought I was it might bring her back to reality. She leaned forward and touched my hand with her index finger. Suddenly, she sprang back in horror liked the surprised shower victim in *Psycho*. Her grandmother hugged her as she began to whimper.

"You ain't Jesus," she slobbered.

"That's right," I said. "I'm a counselor. I'm here to help you."

"No you ain't. You're a plastic Jesus."

I leaned back, shocked. I felt cold and clammy, like I had when I had a near miss with a semi. "Let me call the nurse," I said to her grandmother.

She nodded. The nurse came, gave Felicia a pill to help her sleep, and the grandmother wobbled out the door.

I knew when the psychiatrist arrived mid-morning, Felicia would be given an evaluation and prescribed medication to alleviate her symptoms. I also knew Felicia would become a product of the revolving door system, but most of all, I knew Felicia was right. Even in her state of mind, she had the insight to see beyond my white coat, to see, at some level, my own plasticity. I resigned from my job as counselor and wondered how many other counselors out there were plastic but would continue in their roles.

Practical Jokes

We live in a football-crazed society, and I am not sure how someone can actually live and not get caught up in all the hoopla. Whether it's high school, college, or the pros, I would venture to say that football has become a religion, at least part of the year. When our family gathers for holidays or reunions, we do not discuss religion. Now, however, we do not discuss football because like our respective religions, we have our loyalties and opinions, and more often than not, they do not mesh. I, too, have become somewhat absorbed with football, but my interest lies mainly with the Seminoles at Florida State University, where I earned a graduate degree even though I was raised a Georgia Bulldog, had friends and relatives who were Gators (though not good friends), Tar-heals, War Eagles, Hurricanes, Volunteers, Crimson Tide, among others.

I have Seminole t-shirts, sweat shirts, cups (mainly those nice plastic ones people toss in the trash—my dad collects them, runs them through the dishwasher, and they're germ free and good again—nice stocking stuffers at Christmas), pens, pencils, a Paperweight, a blanket, and most recently a tie I received as a gift from two good friends. What made this tie so special to me was first it was "my" team, but second it's because our good friends Casey and Paul hate my team because their team, The Tennessee Volunteers, in the state I migrated to, has never been a powerhouse of the South.

I used to have a flag, which flew in football season on a pole attached to our house, but one night a devout crusader from a rival team stole the flag and the pole. My neighbors, mainly football neutrals and therefore lost, shook their heads in disgust at my calling the police, filing a report, and demanding a police officer patrol the area at night after I hung my new flag.

Most recently, someone stole my pewter tag off the front of my Jeep, leaving me disgusted and ready to move from the state. I suspected a friend playing a practical joke, but Matt wouldn't admit a thing. For three days, off and on, I analyzed who might have taken the tag. I knew whoever did it wasn't really a thief at heart. First, the pewter tag was screwed into the bumper with thick screws. It would have taken a good five minutes to remove them and make off with my tag. But the perpetrator had taken the time to put the screws back into the bumper. Not smart really because that indicated to me that the criminal was a friend playing a joke. Also, the crime took place during daylight in front of my office, where hundreds come and go. I knew that someone must have seen something, but no one admitted seeing a thing. It may seem paranoid, but I know these fans stick together, especially when it's against a rival of which they're deeply jealous.

More often than not, that instinctive paranoia proved to be justified at the annual Christmas luncheon, where entering the restroom by the cafeteria, I found Xeroxed copies of my tag taped to walls above the urinals. Still, no one said a word.

After the President made a speech, Emily, the chair of the Christmas luncheon committee, stood to recognize those who had assisted. At the end of her speech, she made the announcement that Santa had left only one gift under the tree—for me. Opening the gift, I found my tag while the room roared with laughter. When I returned to my office, I had an email waiting with an attachment. The email was from a bogus address ("your team sucks") and when I opened the attachment, I found pictures of various employees' cars sporting my tag.

I do not recall playing practical jokes or being the object of a practical joke in the flatlands/swamplands of Georgia. Sure, I heard jokes and told jokes, but it was only after I moved to the hills that I began to notice this cultural phenomenon. The first time I witnessed this was when my friend and neighbor Paul played a joke on my wife. Our dog, Harper Lee, was visiting the vet to be "fixed." She was in heat, and town dogs (strays which drifted around town eating from dumpsters and knocking over trashcans in people's yards because there was no leash law, no dog catcher) began coming around. Though Harper herself has no blue bloodline, my wife would not have her breeding with one of the mangy town dogs. Harper had been at the vet's clinic all day and was to spend the night. My wife was worried about her dog and kept asking if she should call. I assured her if there was a problem the vet would call us. Pacified, she continued her weekly cleaning routine, and having completed my chores, I walked over to Paul and Casey's house next door to visit.

Paul forewarned me of his prank as he dialed the number. Disguising his voice, he pretended to be the vet.

"Ms. Julia?" he asked.

"Yes," Julia said.

"This is Dr. Martin at the clinic."

My wife, her voice shaky, asked, "Is everything all right?"

"Oh, yes," he answered. "I didn't mean to alarm you. We have not completed the procedure yet because once we began, we found Harper was pregnant."

"What?" I could hear my wife's raised voice as Paul held the phone a little distance from his ear.

"Yes, Ma'am, I know you must be excited. By the looks of the fetuses, I'd say they might be Great Danes."

"What?" This time, her voice was nearer to a scream.

I heard the screen door slam and saw Julia standing on the porch looking for me. "Hold on." She covered the phone.

She saw me on my neighbors' porch and yelled. "Come here!"

Playing along, I sprinted over. "What's the matter?"

"Harper's pregnant. The vet says the puppies might be Great Danes."

I shook my head. "How can he tell that?"

"Well, he is a vet. He knows those things."

"Is he absolutely sure?"

"Dr. Martin. My husband wants to know if you're absolutely sure."

Julia nodded.

"Ask him if he's really Dr. Martin or if he's a neighbor playing a prank." I smiled.

Julia knew then. She screamed at Paul that she would kill him, turned the portable phone off, and walked toward his house. He laughed till he choked, and Casey reassured Julia she had nothing to do with it. Julia swore she would get him back. To this day, she hasn't, but having lived with her all these years, I know she doesn't forget those sorts of things and will get him back.

Two days had not passed after the dog prank when Bill came to my office to tell me about a practical joke he'd played on his ex-wife's family. He said he knew I would appreciate it. I did not quite understand why he would think that, except I often used humor in my dealings with people and telling stories. Bill looked like a professional wrestler. He sat across from me and told me he hated his ex-wife's family.

"They're just stupid," he said. "They sit around, eating and watching TV all day and night. They don't work and live day to day thinking they'll win the lottery. They spend part of their welfare check on lottery tickets, and when they get into a financial bind, they sell some of their junk in yard sales or at flea markets."

"That's a shame," I said.

"I knew after a while I could not live my life like that. I knew there was something better, so I got out. They were so mad at me when I left that they threatened lawsuits, but I knew they wouldn't sue me, because they're too damned lazy. I made up my mind that I would get them, though."

I nodded.

"About two weeks after I left, I disguised my voice and called from my cell phone in my truck just down the road from their trailer. Told them I was the manager at the grocery store and that they had won a thousand dollars worth of free groceries. I could hear them laughing and hollering. Dorine's mama screamed that their luck was changing. I gave them specific instructions. They were to come to the store immediately, fill their buggies, let the cashier ring it all up, and then tell the cashier to call me, the manager, so I could write it off.

They bought it. I sat in my truck, which was hidden from their view, and waited for them to come pouring out of the trailer. It didn't take long. They piled into their twenty-year-old Oldsmobile and spun out of the clay driveway, leaving clouds of smoke. Their car hit the pavement so hard, the muffler came loose and dragged behind. Then I eased out after they were out of sight and drove to the grocery store."

At this point, I was laughing. Though part of me felt this joke a bit cruel, I supposed I was laughing because it could've been me. I would have fallen for it, too.

"You should have seen them running in the grocery store. First exercise they'd probably had in years. They grabbed buggies and threw the items in so fast, I thought some of them might explode. When their buggies were filled, they stood in line. You could see the cashier was getting nervous about scanning that much stuff. They followed the directions, and after the cashier had rung everything up, they hollered they'd won—for her to get the manager. I had hidden by the greeting card rack near the registers, so I could see. Well, when he got over to the cash register, he was about as stunned as them, and boy were they mad—cursing and stomping around. He threatened to call the police. They stormed out of the grocery store so fast, they nearly knocked a few people down."

"That's amazing," I said. "Did they ever know?"

"No, I never told them. I started to but figured they get a gun and come after me."

I laughed a bit more, but the initial humor had dissipated. I only continued to laugh so he would not get angry at me for not laughing. I felt more afraid that this was a guy I didn't ever want to cross. I was relieved, only briefly, when he changed the subject.

"You like football?"

"Sure do," I said.

"Maybe we can go to a Tennessee game."

There was a thump in my chest. I maintained eye contact, didn't flinch, and said, "That might be fun."

I never went to a football game with Bill, though I did go to a Tennessee game—several, in fact. As with religion, I have learned with age that one should keep his football opinions to himself. It's safer.

Snakes

I've been afraid of snakes at least as far back as the third grade. I guess that a fear of snakes can be healthy if you run up on a poisonous one, but my wife suggested I do something to overcome this fear. She said this after I ran off the road to avoid running over a snake slithering across the road. Some may think that odd, but I had always heard a snake could wrap itself around your wheels and bite you when you get out of the car. Of course, I thought this was logical. What was not logical was what Julia's best friend's husband Rick had done when he flipped his utility vehicle to prevent running over a squirrel.

Nevertheless, I agreed with my wife, which is also quite frequently a healthy choice for me to make. To help overcome the fear, I read a Crews novel set in rural Georgia during a rattlesnake roundup, and late one night I watched a documentary on a snake handling church in Alabama. I thought that if I could find a church like that, I might go and see if I could be in the same room with the people holding snakes and dancing around. Then I thought if I mastered that, I might even see if I could get the spirit and dance with snakes.

After watching the documentary, I took some liquid cold

medicine. It knocked me out rather fast, and I was wrapped up in the flannel sheets in our poster bed. Even though the temperature inside the house was in the seventies with the central heating unit running constantly, it still felt cold. About two-thirty in the morning, I awoke to Julia's screaming at me. Apparently after hearing a knock on the door in my dream, I opened the door to be confronted with snakes all over the stoop. In my battle with the snakes, I must have knocked Julia right off the bed.

I got out of bed, said I was sorry, stumbled through the house, and poured a glass of eggnog, a wintry drink that really doesn't create warmth. I sipped it slowly and looked around the room. For a moment, I believed snakes were in the house, but the more conscious I became, the more I knew this was not true and the more I felt I shouldn't have taken as much cold medicine as I had.

"To hell with snakes," I mumbled to myself in the kitchen. I decided not only would I avoid reading novels or stories about snakes, but also I wouldn't even watch them on television anymore. Sometimes it's more trouble than it's worth to overcome a fear, and like I said, fear can be healthy. I also knew that my fear of snakes was not without reason, since I had been bitten once, nearly bitten several times, and had heard snake stories all my life from relatives who were also afraid of snakes.

The first negative snake encounter I had was when I was eight. Show and tell at school was a big deal. The more interesting, the better. I found a small nonpoisonous garden snake that I put into a cricket container a fisherman would use. I lugged the snake to school in a Scooby-Doo lunch box and when my time came to participate, my fellow classmates were awestruck when I pulled the small, writhing critter out and laid it on the linoleum floor. My teacher, too, was excited and staggered to the back of the room, commanding me in a pleasant way: "*Please* put the snake back in the container."

Of course, being the obedient third grader I was, I followed her command and grabbed the snake to put it back in the cricket jar. As I did, I felt a sharp snag in the palm of my hand. The snake in, I looked at my palm and noticed the blood spots and shouted, "I've been bit."

"Let me see," she said, taking my hand. "Oh dear, looks like you *have* been bitten. Let's go to the principal's office and see the nurse." My classmates oohed and aahed, and the teacher nearly yanked my arm from its socket and dragged me down the hall. The principal knew the garden snake was not poisonous and released it in a cornfield behind the school. The nurse patched my palm with some ointment and a bandage, and I was directed to leave snakes alone in the future, but specifically not to bring any to school. I was afraid the principal would call my mother who would be horrified at what I had done. She, too, was afraid of snakes, partly because she had opened the washing machine to put in a load of laundry only to find a four-foot-long black snake curled and asleep and partly because her mother had been beaten by a snake.

Now, a snakebite is one thing, but being beaten by a snake is something else altogether and something I wasn't sure I believed. My grandmother, though, told the story when we were children, and even as an adult so many years later, I asked her if that story she had told was true. "Yes, that was true," she said. "We found a coach whip snake in the barn and it chased me, caught me, wrapped around my leg, and flung itself up and down, whipping me." Of course, my grandmother also talked about the hoop snake that bit its own tail and rolled down the road like a tire. I had never seen anything like that, and never want to, but I had no reason to doubt what she said. After all, she never drank, and my father-in-law, too, said he had seen them over the years when he was a forester. He didn't drink either. Of course, the heat and humidity of the South can cause people to hallucinate; nevertheless, I did believe them.

Growing up in an area of the country that has so many different types of snakes makes you always on the lookout, mainly looking at the ground, but snakes can swim and snakes can climb. One of my aunts had been bitten by a water moccasin when she was swimming in the river, and I had been chased by a water moccasin in a creek, where I had been wading and scooping up tadpoles to raise into frogs in my aquarium. While scooping tadpoles with a mesh fishing net, I noticed something out of the corner of my eye swimming back and forth and coming toward me. When I focused, I saw the snake and began high stepping toward the bank. Once on the bank, I half-turned my head, looking back; the snake came onto the bank as well and kept on coming. I don't think I looked back again. I ran all the way home, slamming the door behind me, not that a closed door will keep a snake outside. If snakes want inside, they'll get in. We spent summers in a lake cabin in north Florida, and once while sleeping on the top bunk bed, I saw a snake slithering right across the living room floor. My siblings and I screamed, and my dad came and killed the snake.

It was only when I was a teenager that I realized snakes could climb. My uncle shot a five-foot-long oak snake out of a tree at a family picnic. Since we were playing around the chicken coop, the snake had climbed the tree and was attempting to drop onto the tin roof of the chicken coop to either eat the baby chicks or the unhatched eggs. I was stunned to learn snakes could climb.

It seemed all I could do to keep a lookout on the ground for snakes, constantly scanning the earth like radar. One afternoon a friend from high school went with me to a state park. We had decided to get some exercise by walking on the nature trail. The state maintained the trail, which wound its way next to a river, through a swamp, and up steep embankments that seemed to belong to a geographic location other than the flatlands of South Georgia. As we walked, I scanned constantly, never admitting how paranoid I was of snakes.

For several miles I never saw a snake. I had always heard snakes were afraid of humans and unless you provoked them or scared them, they would normally just slide away. Of course, people are going to say something like that to alleviate fears and keep people calm, and I know snakes serve their purpose on this earth; I just wish they would serve their purpose away from me. Nevertheless, I was cautious. Nearing the end of the trail, we came to a shelter. The roof was made of hay, and the posts and beams were hand hewn pine trees. I sat on the picnic table and smoked while my friend stood away from the shelter to avoid my smoking.

"Can you come here?" she asked.

I was relaxed, inhaling and exhaling slowly and trying to cool off. "Why?"

"Just come here," she said.

"I'm sort of enjoying myself here. I'd rather not move. Are you ready to go or something?"

"No, but I want you to come over here now," she said, a

little more firmly than usual.

I noticed her eyes move toward the ceiling and then back at me. I tilted my head ever so slightly upward and saw a six-foot-long rattlesnake uncoiling himself from one of the pine beams and hanging not three feet from my head. I reacted instantly. I leaped from the picnic table, screaming profanity, and landed in the dirt several feet from the shelter. My friend was laughing. "I've never seen anyone jump that far."

As I jumped to my feet, still cursing and feeling my heartbeat in my throat, the snake plopped on the picnic table, coiled, and began shaking its rattles. We ran several feet away, looked back, and the rattling stopped. I knew rattlesnakes could jump twice their length. I had heard it and once saw one leap in the middle of a dirt road. My friend continued to laugh, and I tried to regain my composure, wondering if a friend would have waited instead of just telling me a big rattlesnake was about to fall onto my head.

Another friend of mine was known to play practical jokes on fellow employees at the motel/restaurant/gas station/gift shop situated by the interstate. Such a job for a high school student was easy money, though the hours were often long. My friend would take the rubber snakes out of the gift shop and hide them when no one was watching. I was the lucky recipient of his tricks one night. I had stepped into the kitchen to get a cup of coffee. I returned to operate the manual cash register and stood sipping my coffee and waiting for a customer. When a local customer finally approached the register, I keyed in his ticket amount. When the register flew open, the rubber snake lay jiggling, and I fell back against the wall, cursing and spilling hot coffee all over my starched white shirt. Back then, people did not sue over spilled coffee.

The worst prank he ever played on a fellow employee, however, was with the cook, an elderly black woman with a mysterious heart condition. She reached underneath the grill for a butcher knife, grabbed it, and noticed the rubber snake. She screamed loud and long, and I ran from the register toward the kitchen, worried she might be having one of her heart spells. She came running out of the kitchen and into the dining hall, still screaming and waiving the butcher knife. Her stout, solid body knocked me down, and she ran right out the door into the parking lot. Customers stopped eating and were shocked, but my friend laughed until the owner came out of his office and asked what was going on. Everyone, including me, clammed up and said nothing.

As the flashes of past snake experiences came to an end, and I flipped the channels on the television remote, I landed on a movie advertisement about a giant python in the Congo—pure and simple fiction for someone in America. I covered up with the afghan and decided to watch it. I knew I wouldn't be able to go back to sleep.

Following Willie

When I was twelve, I worked for one day in tobacco. I wanted the job because it paid twenty dollars a day, and I had figured on paper how all those twenties would add up to hundreds by the end of the summer. When a friend of mine told me that Mister Edgar White was hiring, I felt excited and dialed his number with confidence. Mr. White said, "Sure. Pick you up at six. Be out by the road."

My father raised his eyebrows when I told him who I would be working for and asked if I was sure I would rather not mow grass for elderly women in the church. I had mowed grass during the summer and didn't make that much money. Mom, on the other hand, said I would not last a day in the field. I knew otherwise, and besides, money can be a motivator.

Rubbing the sleep out of my eyes, I darted out the door into the humid June morning wearing jeans, tennis shoes, and a t-shirt. A dirty, rusty brown truck caked with mud screeched to a halt by the curb, and a thick black hand reached out to pull me into the truck bed. "Thanks," I said.

"You ever picked tobacco?" The man intensely stared at me, a yellow film floating in his eyes.

"No sir," I said. "But I learn quick. I never knew division, but I made a A on my first test." I told him my name, but he smiled and said he knew who I was.

"I'm Willie," he said. "These two here," he paused, pointing at two heavy black women who looked like tree stumps, "is my girls." They nodded, and I wondered if they would be able to pick tobacco because they looked so thick and helpless. I glanced around the bed of the truck, and other blacks surrounded me. I felt a chill and didn't know if it was the change from my air-conditioned bedroom to the outside humidity or the realization that I was, for the first time, a minority.

The ride to the field was silent and boring like a funeral home, and we drove down a two- lane dirt path lined with longleaf pines. Finally, the path opened into a clearing of tobacco plants, neatly aligned in rows leading as far as I could see, and the truck came to a stop next to a then antique John Deere tractor with a trailer in tow. Everyone began to pile out and take their respective seats, not saying a word, but I sat on the tailgate dangling my legs till I heard Mr. White slam the driver's door.

"What the hell you doin' boy?" One eye stared straight at me, and the other one wandered up toward the pines. "Get your ass on the trailer."

"Yes sir," I said. "My name is—"

Mr. White interrupted. "I don't give a shit who you are. You just do your job."

He jumped on the tractor's seat, cranked it, and it spewed choking smoke out of a rusted pipe on the hood. Willie motioned me next to him, and I took a seat, my hands trembling.

I had hoped for a lesson, some training, like I had received when Miss Etta had hobbled down the steps from her screened porch to show me my lawn mower blades were too low and were skinning her grass, but I quickly followed Willie's lead pulling the sticky tobacco leaves off the stalk as fast as I could. After we had cleared two rows, one on each side of the trailer, we reached the end of the field, and the tractor made a semi-circle heading back in the same direction, but the tractor came to a halt. Mr. White jumped off.

"Boy, that ain't worth a shit!" he yelled, his good eye scanning the row we had just picked. Leaves stuck out in spots all along our row like hairs missed during a shave. Stalks were all that remained on Willie's girls' row. "You get up there and drive the damned tractor!"

I jumped off the trailer. "But, Mr. White…"

"Don't tell me you can't drive a tractor either. Any idiot can drive a tractor."

I climbed up, turned the ignition. I didn't know how to drive a tractor, and although I didn't really know how to crank one either, I had watched my parents crank cars for years and figured I could do it. There was only one problem. I could not see over the bubble hood. I could not keep the tractor within the ruts and ran over two rows of tobacco plants.

"Stop, dammit," I heard over the sputtering sounds of the pipe. Mr. White was sprinting to my left, pointing at the brake, but my leg would not reach it. He grabbed hold of the fender and flung himself next to me, almost pushing me off, and slammed his muddy boot onto the pedal. The tractor came to a jolting halt. "Get off," he said. His face was red, and his eye glared at me; a blood vessel jumped around under the skin of his forehead. "You're pitiful. Just get on the trailer and do what you can."

I felt bad. I had caused him a lot of problems, but I was also mad because he had yelled and cursed at me. My parents did not even do that. The preacher yelled, but he never cursed unless it was a quote. I fought back the tears and turned my racing heartbeat into focused energy and plucked leaves of tobacco as fast as I could. At lunch, everyone unloaded, wiping sweat and talking about how hot it was. I ate a peanut butter and jelly sandwich and drank ice water out of a Bell jar underneath an oak covered with Spanish moss next to the barn where others were stringing tobacco on sticks and hanging them to dry on racks. After our break, we worked till the sun began to go down when Mr. White drove the tractor out of the field and stopped next to his Ford truck. He handed out twenties from a wad and gave me one. "Well," he said, "I think you got the hang of it. See you back in the morning."

I did not respond. Whether I was still angry or more tired than I had ever been in my life, I don't know. When I got home, I bathed, scrubbing till my skin was red, but the tobacco stains remained. I nodded at the dinner table, and the next morning when Mr. White's truck horn blew and my dad came to wake me, I faked sick. My eager little brother jumped up and begged to go in my place. Off he went, and I felt sorry for him and wanted to say something but did not.

At the end of the second day, Mr. White had told my brother not to come back, and on the third morning, I awoke before dawn, rubbing the matter out of the corner of my eyes. I stared out the window as headlights came nearer our house. As each vehicle passed, I felt relieved like finding out a perceived snake was only a stick. But each time another vehicle approached, another sinking feeling overwhelmed me because I did not know what I would do if Mr. White's truck stopped since I had not technically been fired, nor had I officially quit. I watched for an hour, and when the sun had risen, I knew Willie and his girls were pulling leaves, and I was free to go back to sleep.

Years later, I drove home one Christmas and made a rare decision to attend church services with my parents. As I stood, holding a hymnbook and singing "Precious Memories" off key, I noticed a somewhat familiar face a few rows down. It was Mr. White. His hair had thinned, his skin looked like a crumpled brown lunch sack, but he looked cleaner in his blue suit than he had when I had worked for him that day. I wondered if he had found religion near the end of his life because of the awareness of the nearing end, or if he had truly changed in some way. When services were over, I opted not to speak to him first, but to wait and see if he recognized, remembered the mean things he had said to me. The thought of talking to him made me feel uneasy. As the crowd shuffled toward the exit like cattle, his good eye looked at me and his head nodded, not from any recognition, but from politeness, and I chose to remain silent.

UFOs

When I finally saw a UFO, I satisfied a desire inspired by my Uncle Raymond, who once saw one late at night, driving on a rural Georgia road on his way home from work. At family reunions, kids would gather around, their stomachs full of fried foods and their brown eyes sparkling, and listen to stories. Uncle Raymond's deep and booming voice would recount to us the lights of the ship that followed him.

"I was driving home and noticed lights from a UFO that hovered over my truck and followed me. It didn't make no sound, and it was fast." He spoke slowly and surely, more convincing than a preacher.

"Were you scared?" one cousin asked.

"Nah, boy," Uncle Raymond thundered, chuckling. "They're just trying to study us."

"What do they look like?" another cousin asked.

"They ain't green like they show them in the movies," he said, squinting his eyes and shifting in his lawn chair. "They are gray and have big dark eyes. They don't talk; they communicate with their minds."

"How do you do that?" I asked.

"We ain't learned how," he responded. "But people think

you have to get real quiet and concentrate real hard." Uncle Raymond hadn't read parapsychological literature. He told us that to keep us quiet, so we wouldn't disturb the older folks, who were napping in lawn chairs till time to eat again.

"I'd like to see one," I said.

"Well," he speculated, arching his brows. "You just might see one some night."

"You really think so?" I excitedly asked.

"Sure," he said. "They're all over the place."

With those words, my eyes turned heavenward at night, looking. Occasionally, I saw a shooting star, which I thought might be a UFO because it was quieter and faster than the jets that roared in the night sky. Of course, two different relatives had told me the meaning of shooting stars. My grandfather said they were an omen that someone in the family would die within a short period of time. An aunt said they meant good luck if you closed your eyes, wished, and didn't tell anyone. Bases covered, I wished no one would die and, if the shooting star was a UFO, it would come visit me. My wishes were realized when I finally saw a UFO while I was working at a military base in college.

The fog was thick as I drove down the highway toward the base, making it tough to see anything in the road. I had slept all afternoon, but my body was telling me to go back to sleep. Matter floated in both my eyes, and I kept rolling my eyes and squinting. I worried I might total my car, and I feared my insurance would not cover the damage.

As I entered the gate, I stopped and spoke to Master Sergeant Brian Todd, chief of Security Police for the eleven at night to seven in the morning shift. Stout and bleary eyed, Todd downed coffee and cream-filled doughnuts to stay awake. "I think it's gonna be a slow night; want a doughnut?"

"No." I had heard of Todd's practical jokes. He had squeezed out the chocolate from doughnuts, melted Ex-lax in the microwave, and refilled the doughnuts for his subordinates. "Better go. Got a lot of studying to do." I waved, pulled away, and knew it would be a slow night; it always was. It simply amazed me that I got paid so much to do so little. I speculated that the government was the place to work. I also knew I wouldn't study. I never did, as my transcripts so gloriously reflect. What I did do was drink coffee, thick and syrup-like, and while I was not supposed to fall asleep, I often just rested.

I parked and walked through the mist toward the beige World War II barracks turned into offices. I entered the office and glanced at the layered blue smoke hanging near the fluorescent ceiling lights. Betty, the three in the afternoon to eleven at night billeting clerk, smoked like a locomotive, and without looking away from her Harlequin romance novel said, "Hey."

"Hey," I said back. I counted the money in the cash register, which seemed a waste of time because no one would bother stealing thirty dollars in change and bills. "Money checks out," I told Betty.

"Okay, see you tomorrow night," she muttered, stuffing her book into her plastic purse.

I emptied ashtrays, straightened chairs, turned the TV channel to CNN, and completed the paperwork, various forms with numbers and acronyms, none of which I knew the meaning of. Finished, I sat on the sofa and propped my feet on the coffee table, listening to the slow hiss of the steam radiators that filled the room with stuffiness, and I began to relax.

I opened my eyes when I heard a vehicle pass and glanced at the clock: three o'clock in the morning. I staggered to the bathroom and splashed cold water on my face. I realized I was still asleep, so I walked outside to breathe the cold night air. That's when I saw the UFO. It hovered just above the Officer's Club. Colorful lights flashed around its circular shape, and I could hear no sounds. I blinked a couple of times before I realized it was not a figment of my imagination. I bolted toward the building and locked the door. I pulled the phone under the desk with me to call Todd. A juvenile reaction? Maybe. The way I figured it, there were two possibilities. Either the UFO belonged to the United States Air Force as some TV programs had suggested, or it was alien. If it was ours, I felt sure I was not supposed to see it. If it was not of this planet, I felt sure they could see me because they were obviously more intelligent than we were to be able to build such a ship and fly it to our planet. I dialed the phone.

"Sergeant Todd, you awake?"

"Of course." The liar cleared his throat.

"You ain't gonna believe this."

"What is it?"

"There's a UFO hovering over the Officer's Club."

A brief pause followed. Finally, Todd said, "There's some regs about pulling pranks on military personnel."

"I swear to God I'm not making this up."

Not convinced, Todd tried a threat. "I'll have to report this to the Command Post."

"I'm not lying." I had not been the boy who cried wolf in years.

"Okay," he said. "I'm on my way."

I stayed under the desk, and when I heard the door rattling, I peeked out to make sure it was Todd. I felt more comfortable because if there was going to be an abduction, I knew they would take him since he knew what all the acronyms meant.

"I don't see nothing," he said. Fear flowed through my body at the thought of losing my high paying government job. Walking into the fog and looking up into the night sky, I was surprised to see the UFO still hovering.

"There," I pointed, feeling job security.

"You've got to be kidding." He shook his head.

"You don't see it?"

"Yeah, I see your UFO. Only it's the base water tower."

I swallowed hard. The thick fog shrouded the steel legs of the water tower, and the lights that flashed as a warning to incoming F-4s and F-16s seemed distant. The more I gaped, the more the UFO became terrestrial. I wondered where the unemployment office was located. "Sorry," I whispered. "It damned sure looked like a UFO."

"There's gonna be trouble now. Command Post has to wake the Base Commander. It's policy."

"Can't you stop them before they do?"

"I radioed them on the way. I'm sure they already have. They take these reports seriously."

Sullenly, I walked back toward the office.

"You see anything else, give me a call." Todd's sarcasm was not impressive.

My shift ended as the sun burned away the night fog. I skipped class and lay in bed, tossing, turning, and waiting on a phone call that never came. Visions of being fired by the Billeting manager, a retired Green Beret, and being blessed out by the Base Commander, a General obsessed with neatness, were almost too much to bear. By the time I arrived at the base the next night, my hands already trembled, and I had not even had coffee. Betty was again reading a Harlequin. "Heard about your UFO," she chuckled without looking up. "I reckon Sergeant Todd got you."

The relief I felt was better than a laxative when constipated. I got to keep my government job and continued to pay for an education I cared little for at that time. I may not have learned a great deal in college, but working at the base taught me how to keep my mouth shut. Some nights, I still look heavenward and hope to see a UFO.

The Dinghy

In college, I went to see a therapist for math anxiety and to get hypnotized into passing my algebra class, but all she wanted to do was past life regressions (and take my money, I suspected), which I thought was bunk. She diagnosed me with what she called water fever, saying it seriously and softly like a nun whispering vespers while rubbing my palm.

"You died tragically in your last life," she said, holding my hand while her turquoise yin-yang bracelets clanked against my Eddie Bauer watch.

"How?" I quizzed.

"In water," she said, bringing her heavily painted seaweed eyelashes together.

"Oh," I nodded, and even though I thought she was full of it, I did fear she might know my thoughts.

"I believe you have what we call water fever. Until you can get beyond your fear of water, you shouldn't go near it."

"What about bathing?" I was being sarcastic, but she did not seem bothered.

"Sure, silly, just don't completely fill the tub." She winked.

I paid her, drove home, studied for my math final, and

flunked. It was not until my senior year, when I finally passed algebra from practice and study, that I could reflect on my naiveté in thinking I could get hypnotized into passing math as if knowledge originates osmotically.

Years later, when Jamie, a friend from college, invited me to vacation at his family's home on Tybee Island, Georgia, near Savannah, I hesitated, in contrast to my usual spontaneity, because of jellyfish stings, near attacks from gators, and malignant skin cancer from years of sunning bathed in Wesson oil, which was before sun block.

"Ah, come on," he begged.

An accelerated heartbeat and sweat beads formed as I remembered being eight years old and fishing for catfish in Hodge's Pond when my childhood friend Felton rocked the boat, spilling us into the oil-colored water. The floating alligators looked like logs. They sank below, and I knew as I swam like Aqua Man toward shore that the gators sensed lunch. After all, I had heard people say they had thrown live chickens into the water, watching them flap and squawk till they disappeared with a swoosh on the surface of the pond. Fortunately, Mr. Hodges noticed our spill and launched himself in his Bass troller to rescue Felton who could not swim and clung, screaming and kicking, to the underside of boat.

"Well," I stuttered to Jamie.

Listening to Jamie's whining about how we could fish, drink, and talk (knowing he would talk while I would listen) made me sigh, and I gave in, rationalizing the trip would do me good. Maybe I would have a positive experience with water like I did as a child during toilet training when I would aim at Cheerios tossed in the bowl by my dad.

"See you next week then," he said.

"Yeah, unless I change my mind," I replied.

"You better not change your mind," he demanded.

"I won't," I said, knowing I would certainly think about it, but wouldn't because of unconscious guilt instilled in childhood by Baptist ministers.

The next week, when I left inland Atlanta in my Mustang, I let both windows down, since my air conditioner did not work, and drove sixty-two miles per hour, knowing the Georgia State Patrol would not give me a ticket unless I was doing eight miles per hour above the speed limit.

Several pit stops, Cokes, and cheese crackers later, I smelled the faint salt in the air, which tended to dry and soothe smog-infested, inner-city sinuses. I wondered if I could deduct the trip on taxes, calling it a health necessity, but figured I would not have enough documentation come audit time.

I pulled into the dirt drive, dust rose behind me, and Jamie came onto the flaky green cement porch. My Mustang shook like Elvis and backfired when I switched it off. Firmly shaking hands, Jamie and I made small talk about the weather till he offered me a Corona with lime. "'Preciate it," I said, grabbing a duffle bag and following him inside the 1930's Chicago-style bungalow, which looked out of place alongside new vinyls on stilts.

We sat in rockers, listening to the waves crash against the shore and sipping Coronas. "I thought you'd back out," Jamie said.

"I can't believe you'd think that," I lied. "How's your family?"

"Dysfunctional as usual," he smirked. "It's amazing I turned out as good as I did."

Hmm. I figured someone who knew he was dysfunctional and would not admit it was pretty dysfunctional. "You done any fishing since you've been here?"

"Nah, I set some crab traps and caught four. Thought we'd cook them for dinner."

"Sounds good to me." I imagined the tender, white meat, dipped in a lemon butter sauce, and my stomach rumbled.

"I thought we'd take the old row boat out," Jamie said staring at the sea.

Something about the word "old" did not please me. "How old is it?"

"Been in the family for three generations. We used to take it out all the time." Jamie pointed. "I thought we'd go over to that island and do some fishing till the sun goes down."

"Is it safe?" I gripped the rocker's handles, not knowing if the Corona was that strong a beer, or if I felt panic about going where God only knew what lurked below.

Jamie chuckled till he coughed and spit phlegm into the spur-laced yard. "You just need to loosen up; enjoy life."

Nothing annoyed me more than for someone to tell me to loosen up; I considered myself pretty laid-back. "I do enjoy life," I hissed. "I just wanted to know if this boat was safe; that's all."

"I took it out all through childhood and never had a problem," he snorted.

"Well, okay."

"When you finish your beer, we'll get going," Jamie said, walking inside and bringing back salt water rods and reels and a tackle box. "I'll put these in the boat."

I chugged the rest of the beer, mostly foam, and walked

down the plank sidewalk that connected to the dock. Glaring sun, sea breezes, and salt water had cracked the wood, causing splinters to stick up and stub my toes since they curled over the edges of my K-Mart flip-flops. The dunes of white sand and sparsely grown saw grass seemed a desert atmosphere, except for sea sprays, like giant squirts of Afrin nasal spray.

Jamie tossed dirty cups and potato chip bags into an oil barrel trashcan tied to a dock post. Afterward, the two-seater boat looked relatively clean. "Get in," he said. "And sit there." The boat teetered when I stepped in the front and plopped on the bench. Jamie tossed in the fishing supplies and a cooler of beer. Stepping into the boat, Jamie untied the rope, pressed an oar against the dock pole, and shoved us off.

The first fifteen minutes of staring into the dark Atlantic bothered me. My hands were sweaty, and I felt seasick, but Jamie talked about the wild horses we might see on the island, which took my mind off the fear. I relaxed and enjoyed watching the yachts and ships in the distance. We rowed past a bobbing red buoy with a dinging bell, reminding me of being called to church as a child. Just as I had become totally at peace, I felt it.

The liquid on my feet was cold and shocking, like when diving into a pool on a scorching day. "Where the hell is this water coming from?" I asked.

I could tell by his wide eyes he had not noticed the water in the boat. "I don't know," he said. "Maybe it splashed in."

"Hell no, it didn't," I snapped. "There ain't no big waves." I looked out for reassurance, not that finding a relatively calm sea would be all that comforting.

"There must be a leak," said Jamie. "There was never a leak before." Searching for a leak, his eyes darted.

"Turn back, damn it," I screamed, gripping the sides of boat. *God almighty*, I prayed, *I'm too damned young to die.* Adrenaline caused random thoughts to swirl into my consciousness like a hurricane spinning and making landfall in a sleepy seaside village. Flashes of wrongs, like the time I put my little brother in the dryer and turned it on, the time I yelled at my mother for making fun of my John Travolta leisure suit, the time I smoked in the church bathroom and the preacher found out, and the times I lusted about Farrah Fawcett, made me shiver and break out in a cold sweat. Lord, one more chance, I begged, and just in case He had not heard my thoughts, I sent them again.

"I'm not turning back," Jamie said. "We're closer to the island than we are the mainland. Don't panic! We'll make it." Jamie no longer glanced at his muscles while he rowed; he just rowed, the oars slapping the water like windshield wipers on high in a rainstorm. I cupped my hands together and scooped water as fast as I could.

"No, No," Jamie said. "Bust a beer bottle on the side and use that." His idea made sense, and when I smashed the bottle, the jagged glass sliced a vein on my wrist. Blood squirted into the sea and boat, and it wasn't until it squirted all over my chest that I realized what was wrong.

"My God," I yelled. "My wrist is cut bad."

"Get that towel out of there, rip it, and tie it tight around your wrist." Jamie nodded toward the compartment in the middle of the boat.

Water was up to our ankles, and the combination of fear and adrenaline put me in high gear; though it seemed forever, I quickly slowed the bleeding to a slow drip. I felt weak, dizzy, and nauseous, but managed to continue to scoop water in the beer bottle using my left hand. Keeping my right arm elevated as much as I could, I began waving and screaming at a nearby yacht. The tanned couple laughed and toasted to us with their martinis. I could not hear them, but I imagined what they were saying: *Oh how cute. Two young fellows rowing in a little wooden boat. I just don't know why they would want to do it the hard way.* Then, my imagination responded: *Can't you see we're in trouble? You drunk fools. There are sharks out here. Big sharks. Why don't you help us?* If my hand had not been throbbing, I would have flipped them a bird.

Just when I thought my water experience could not get worse, I saw a fin. Part of me felt I should not have thought about sharks—that somehow thinking about them made them come. It wasn't a big fin like *Jaws*, but a fin is a fin. "Faster," I yelled. "Shark!"

Jamie's eyes shot toward the water. Your blood must've attracted him. That and the oars slapping the water."

"Great." I kept scooping water.

"We're almost there," Jamie said.

I no longer cared if we made it or not. I did not see the fin; whether it had moved on after not discovering lunch or whether my eyes were blurry from tears, I did not know. I felt catatonic. What brought me back to reality was Jamie's jumping from the boat into the water. I quickly turned, my eyes wide like an owl. "What're you doing?"

"We're close enough in now that I can pull us faster than rowing." Jamie gripped the bow and swam, pulling us along till he could feel the cold ocean floor with his feet. Soon enough, the boat was pulled onto a sand bar. I got out and walked through the water, little waves lapping my feet, and fell in the sand. I sat Indian style, watching tiny crabs scamper out of holes when waves receded and scurry in their holes when waves rushed in, and it occurred to me how cyclical life was and that the psychic from college days was right. Not totally right, of course, but right about my fear. I'd had enough fear of water to last me this life. Rather than brush away my fear of water, I quietly resolved to conquer it.

Jamie pulled the boat off the sandbar and onto the beach. "How you feeling?"

"I'm okay."

"You stay here. I'm gonna see if I can find some help over here."

"No." My voice was firm and calm. "Let's get the stuff and fish. My hand is okay. We can patch the boat's hole with leaves and mud."

Jamie cocked his head. "You've lost your mind, haven't you?"

"No, we've got to do it, you know?"

"Yeah," Jamie squinted. "I think I do."

Woman Thing

When I heard Julia's car screech into the drive, I unlocked the back door. The way she carried her purse, I knew she was down again about her job, and just tinkering with the lock would irritate her. Julia had been caught up in a game, which she was losing through no fault of her own. She wanted to quit, walk out, tell them off, but I had said no time and again because we couldn't survive a month on my salary. Each time Julia expressed her fantasies, I had fantasies of my own: repossessed material possessions, bad credit reports, and bankruptcy. Visions of seedy men coming at ungodly hours to take away what I had convinced myself was mine, even though everything really belonged to some corporate financial ghost, scared me into thoughts of revenge.

The vengeful thoughts produced feelings of guilt, and I saw my preacher from childhood, mopping his beet face with a snot-colored rag, hammering his fist on the pine podium, and screaming about hell. I fanned the preacher away and convinced myself the game would either come to an end, or I would create a new game with my own rules. After all, I rationalized, when people you love hurt, you become the antidote.

The screen door slammed, and Julia threw her purse on the sofa.

"How was your day," I asked, pouring us glasses of chardonnay, which topped the Mad Dog I guzzled in college. I felt stupid and insensitive, but I didn't really know how else to approach the subject.

"How do you think it was?" Julia kicked off her pumps and plopped in an oak Windsor chair at the kitchen table, a flea market find.

"Anything new happen?" I guzzled the wine and poured another.

"Yeah," she smirked. "Etta was talking to her follower Bobbie about me again. Said I was after her job and acted like I already ran the place." Tears welled in her eyes. Jealousy, idle chitchat from empty heads, and rumors had resulted, ironically enough, in reprimands for Julia, first verbal and later written, from Charles, king of the rural phone business.

I had met them all at a Christmas party I didn't want to go to but felt obligated to attend for Julia. Etta was nearing retirement. Passing herself off as the helper to newcomers, she knitted doilies as I imagined Madame Defarge doing in *Tale of Two Cities*, and gave them away—a show of her hypocrisy. Etta had come from poverty, moving up from sharecropper to share owner in the company and acquiring jewelry, which dangled from her sagging skin like shimmering ornaments on a withered Christmas tree.

Bobbie, on the other hand, was named by her mother after the Janis Joplin song right before her mother committed suicide from postpartum depression. Bobbie's father drank a lot and abused her. She trusted no one, and her paranoia resulted in three failed marriages. Heavy make-up, clopping heels, and tight-fitting velour dresses made her look like a show horse named bad childhood.

When Julia had been accused of being fake because she was nice to customers and company employees, I laughed it off, but when they called her a hypocrite, I was furious. Nothing could have been further from the truth. Julia taught Sunday school; she even read the Bible and prayed. I only went to church with her when they had a covered dish supper. I felt if it would help her work situation, I would pray, not to the New Testament's forgive-and-forget God but to the Old Testament's wrathful God who I fantasized would pour out his vengeance on the company like Sodom and Gomorrah.

"Julia, why don't you go see Charles again? Maybe if you were more assertive?"

"Right,"she snorted. "He'll just think I'm whining."

Julia was right, and I couldn't believe I had made such a suggestion. Charles topped them all. An engineer in management—an oxymoron. Just because crisscross wires work together does not mean crisscross people will. Julia told me each time she approached him about Etta and Bobbie, he would lean back in his creaking chair, plop his wingtips on his cherry desk, fold his hands together as if praying, and say, "Honey, it's a woman thing. Men just beat the hell out of each other." King Charles would wink at her, which bothered her and me. Here was an outstanding member of the community. I felt Charles just needed the hell beat out of him. Split his head open and pour some sexual harassment sense into it. But nothing can convince people to change when they don't feel the need.

"Well," I muttered, "What can I do?"

"Listen," Julia said. She gulped her wine and looked

around the room to change the subject. "This house is just too dark. Paneling is out. Maybe we could paint it."

"What?" I chuckled. "You've got to be kidding. It's a rental house."

"Then," Julia demanded: "I am going to do a new flower bed out front. There needs to be something bright around here."

Even the Round-up I had sprayed on the flowerbed didn't curb her desire to grow more flowers. Sometimes I wished Julia were an alcoholic. At least then, I could get her some help. There was no support group for people addicted to flowers, and the damned things were everywhere: Eucalyptus wreaths on the walls, magnolia and iris prints in the kitchen and on the curtains, potted palms in the living room, and close-out Waverly floral wallpaper in the bathroom. Even the plates were a botanical print. "You go on and plant you a flower bed, but we're digging it up when we move; it's a waste of money." I got up and turned on the TV.

"Deal," she said. "One more thing."

"What's that?"

"Don't plan on staying in your job next year. You said I couldn't quit, and I'll accept that, but you need to look for another job. No more podunk towns. I just can't take this anymore."

Julia dragged herself out of the chair, and like a tree in a hurricane, she swayed back and forth down the hall where she would take off her hose, bra, skirt, and blouse, throw on a worn tee-shirt and shorts, and fall on the bed. Part of me wanted to fall on the bed, too. I had no idea who else would hire me since my college GPA was so low. I had only taken the job because it was the only offer I had, but since I had gained more experience, I felt my chances might be better. Résumés, interviews, and another move made me feel nauseous, and I decided if her job-related problems were alleviated, she would feel better—we could stay. Ultimately, the feminist part of Julia would never admit she wanted me to take control and meddle, but I assumed part of her would like the idea. After all, I had opened sealed-tight salsa and jelly jar lids, which she could have easily opened had she tried.

My growling stomach, and knowing Julia wouldn't wake till dawn, pushed me out the door, into my truck, and down the highway—a five year Department of Transportation work in progress where misshapen men, who looked like badly landscaped trees and untrimmed hedges, smoked, kicked gravel, and told jokes instead of paving. Like a programmed robot, my truck made its way to Dewey's while I wondered how I could get even. I pulled alongside the curb in front of Dewey's, and entering the bar and grill, the blues band sang "Minnie the Moocher." I practically swallowed the Dewey burger, a dietician's nightmare, while nursing a beer.

After another beer, I began deciphering the drunken wall scribbling that seems comic during inebriated nights, but on sober days is childish. While part of me thought about murder, I knew I could never commit such a harsh crime. I had even thought about putting rattlesnakes in their mailboxes, but figured that might be indirect murder; besides, I feared snakes more than anything. When I read, "government sucks," on the wall, I knew I had rediscovered a philosophical truth I had all but forgotten, but until recently had no reason to spit out. The awareness set off a mental chain reaction clicking with possibilities, like dominos, and almost simultaneously, I knew the IRS was the one bureaucratic entity I could count on for screwing up their lives, never implicating Julia or me.

When I got home from the pub, I sat on the porch, smoked, and imagined how I could sic the IRS on the evil employees. After plotting my plan of revenge, I decided a good night's sleep would help the plan fall into place, so I collapsed onto the bed. In my dream, I called a toll-free number for the IRS I'd found in the phone book. After anonymously reporting Etta to the IRS for cheating on the capital gains and miscellaneous deductions (including alleged tithes to her church), I reported Bobbie for not reporting child support as additional income and Charles for not including earnings from gambling and fabricating work-related trips and mileage for which he claimed he wasn't reimbursed. The agency bought my story, and I sat back, rubbing my belly and feeling full and satisfied, like I had eaten Tums after a grease-laced Dewey burger. Though I did feel some guilt at first, I rationalized they probably did do what I had accused them of doing simply because most people commit white-collar crime. I also decided I would find King Richard and beat the hell out of him since that was his desire.

Some dreams are fast-paced and some, when you awake, feel like they took forever. This one was slow and repetitive, like when you buy a new tape, but rewind the cassette to hear your favorite song over and over. It seemed weeks before I had any inclination my plan had worked. In the meantime, Julia would drag in, change clothes, and fall asleep night after night. I cooked, cleaned, and handled all financial business like I was on Prozac. Occasionally, Julia would say, "Why are you so happy?" Emphatically, I would say, "Because I love you." "Right," was her somber response. Like a student who has caught a teacher smoking, heard a teacher farting, or found out the demigod had at one time failed a class, I could barely keep the secret.

"Hey!" Julia breezed in the living room with a fresh smile as if she were doing a toothpaste commercial.

"What's up? You win the lottery?"

"You're not going to believe who I ate lunch with!" Julia's eyebrows curved upward, forming an upside-down V. "Etta and Bobbie."

"What?" I dropped my mouth open for a second to appear shocked. "How could you eat lunch with them after all they've done to you?" I felt needed to act more surprised and paranoid, so I paced up and down the floor. "What are they up to?"

"God," Julia said. "I knew you would act this way." She shook her head.

"Well, what happened?"

"Etta came first, see. She said she and Bobbie had this problem they wanted to talk to me about since I had been to college and wanted to know if I would go to Dewey's with them. I wasn't sure but figured whatever. It couldn't get worse, so I agreed."

"So you guys left right then?" I propped my feet on the coffee table.

Julia ran her finger across the TV. "Jeez, this is dusty." She sprinted into the kitchen, projecting her voice. "No, that was early." One of the cabinet doors slammed, and she waltzed back into the living room with a dingy rag in one hand and a can of Pledge in the other. She sprayed the lemon mist onto the rag and started wiping and talking at the same time, a trait I found somehow annoying. "We didn't go till around twelve. Of course we had to pass all those construction workers on the highway, and they had to stop to say hey since they are related or old flames. When we got to Dewey's, we talked about flowers and read the writing on the wall. It wasn't until Bobbie read that government sucks on the wall that they finally got to their reason for inviting me."

"What was their reason for inviting you?" I quizzed even though I knew what was coming and figured Etta and Bobbie accused her of reporting them to the IRS.

Julia lifted books off the mantle, laid them in the Queen Ann chair, and wiped the wood. "Etta's eyes teared, and Bobbie took her shaking hands. She told me the IRS was after her and didn't know why."

Apparently, I thought, they didn't tell her about the anonymous reports. So far so good. Julia looked like a child who had been told she could not go outside and play because of a storm. "Well, can you believe this? They are auditing her for the past seven years and found what they call some discrepancies. They say she owes at least forty thousand in back tax, interests, and penalties. She's going to have to sell her house and rent an apartment. She might even lose some of her retirement, and who could survive on Social Security these days?"

"Wow, that's awful," I said. Secretly, I felt she deserved it. "Sort of serves her right, don't you think?"

"No, it doesn't. How can you say that? Sure, she's a little mean and all, but deep down, she's a good person."

"You're right. How could I be so cold-hearted?" I knew that if Julia found out what I had done, she would not understand.

"I've asked Etta to come over this weekend, and I'm going to go through her records with her and help. After all, I did minor in accounting."

"You're kidding."

"No, I'm not kidding, and that's not all. The IRS is also investigating Bobbie and looking into her previous files because they claimed she might not have included child support. She looks awful."

I almost laughed, but managed to keep the smile to a smirk. "More than usual?"

"Do you have heart?" Her beagle eyes melted my innards.

"Sure, but these two have made our lives miserable, and I think they've got what's coming to them."

"I see your point," she said. "But I also know I've been praying for them, and the Lord works in mysterious ways."

"I guess you're right." I knew God was not at work here.

"I don't know what's gonna happen. If the IRS finds something, I don't know how she'll survive. How's she gonna feed those younguns then? None of her sorry ex-husbands help her at all."

Grimacing, I had not considered the effects this might have on her children. "Maybe they won't find anything."

"Well, if they do and she loses her job, I'll get the church to help. I'm gonna cook supper and take it over there tonight. Can you fix yourself something to eat?"

"I guess," I said as Julia bounced into the kitchen and began rattling pots and pans. I felt stunned that she could forgive and forget so easily and befriend them in such a manner. Somehow, her attitude made it easier on me, like when a classmate in school says your mama wears combat boots, but when you tell your mama, she doesn't care, so you feel better. The scene then flashed to my childhood preacher, who was pointing, huffing and puffing about sin and guilt, and I knew that even though I had done the wrong thing, it had worked out for the best. I felt ashamed and decided to keep quiet about my meddling. As I awoke, rubbing the sleep from eyes, I was relieved it was just a dream, since I probably wouldn't have done all that anyway, but I really felt glad I didn't have to fight King Charles since he was bigger than me. I felt like I had been through enough. I also realized he was right; it was a woman thing. Julia eventually quit and got a better job immediately, making much more money, and we bought our first house.

Birds

I am not a bird hater, but I'm not a bird lover either. Even though I don't understand birdwatchers, I'm not prejudiced against them, but I do have these waves of prejudice against birds. I have come to believe all birds have it in for me. I don't know if my belief is fear from watching Hitchcock's movie as a child or from seeing mockingbirds attack my grandmother and pecking at her head, but I do know it's real.

When I was in college in Georgia, I went to a party at a Philosophy professor's house. People stood, smoking and drinking, in the manicured backyard, and while I listened to an English professor, who also happened to be a nun, pontificate on existential philosophy, a bird perched in a dogwood tree dropped its waste. Whether it was too many beers that had slowed my reaction time or whether I was just simply stunned, I do not know, but I watched as the mess ran all the way down the front of my seersucker shirt.

A few years later in graduate school in Florida, I had parked at the civic center, paid my daily parking fee, and walked half a mile to the Gothic red brick building where I absorbed Russian literature. I was halfway down the sidewalk when a gull dropped its waste into my freshly gelled hair. I had been late to the literature seminar because I had spent fifteen minutes washing my hair with industrial soap in a stained sink. Peers in the seminar wondered why my hair looked like wet straw and didn't believe my story.

When my wife and I bought a house four years ago, I had a lot of work to do. I loved the wood-burning fireplace and chimney, but had a chimney sweeper come and clean it because I feared the house would burn. Upon inspection, the chimney sweeper felt I should install a cap on the chimney to keep out birds. When he had cleaned it, he told me it was evident they had been nesting inside the chimney, so I ran to Home Depot, bought the metal cap and rushed back home so he could install it. When spring came and birds were building nests, the swallows constantly swooped down to the chimney cap and attempted to get in. Part of me felt guilty, but I alleviated those feelings by remembering the mess the chimney man had scraped out. Finally, I just got mad. When I would step outside and onto the deck to grill or to smoke, the swallows would swoop down, screaming at me. My wife Julia had said, "They're not after you. They're catching bugs to eat." I had responded, "I don't give a damn if they're catching bugs or not, but I'm gonna protect myself." I had taken a broom outside with me every time I was going to grill or smoke, and when the swallows swooped, I tried to knock them from the sky. It never worked, but I'm sure my jumping around and swinging the broom in the air gave my neighbors something to talk about. The next spring, the swallows did not return. I suppose they found another neighbor to torment.

Now, though, the wrens are the problem. Last week, the garage door was open, and I noticed these two wrens flying in and out of the garage. Upon closer inspection, I noticed they were building a nest on a shelf where I have a bunch of junk stored. (I say junk, but as soon as I give in to Julia's pleas to throw it away, it will become something I shouldn't have thrown away.) I closed the garage and vowed to keep it shut. My neighbors were outside, and I told them about the nest. They, too, are experiencing a dilemma. Blackbirds have been building a nest in their grill. They have cleaned it, turned on the grill and burned it, but the blackbirds have constructed a new nest by the time they get home from work. They are able to get in through the bottom of the grill. I felt a little better about my wren problem. At least wrens are small birds, song-birds, not big birds that scream like those blackbirds.

That evening after I had closed the garage, I noticed that the rubber piece at the bottom of the garage door had a small section missing on one side. Just then, one of the wrens landed and hopped right through the opening. I knew then that was how the wrens had been getting in and out. Part of me wanted to run them out, clean the nest area, and replace the rubber flap on the bottom of the garage door, but since my wife is with child, I've become, or at least attempted to become, more sensitive. I decided to let the birds stay in their home.

Yesterday morning, I heard all of this racket in the garage. It sounded like birds screaming at each other. At first, I thought the eggs had hatched, but when I peered into the garage, another bird had somehow become trapped, and the wrens were screaming at the new bird, a cardinal, which was screaming right back at them. "Okay," I told Julia. "I decided to let those wrens stay, but I'll be damned if another bird is gonna take up in there." This screaming went on for about an hour. I had opened the garage, but the cardinal couldn't figure how to fly out of the garage even though the door was open, which makes the word birdbrain more real than ever.

I never saw when the cardinal flew out of the garage. I only knew the noise had quieted some. Then, I noticed a half-dollar size white spot on my Jeep hood and wondered if the cardinal or wren had left the spot. I cursed toward the bird nest and thought if it happened again and no other bird was present, I would know the guilty party and would clean house.

Once I backed my Jeep out of the garage, I hosed the spot off and felt a little better. I walked back inside and downed one more cup of coffee before making the fourteen-mile journey to work, which, incidentally, takes about forty minutes with the traffic. There are essentially three routes I drive, varying and depending on time and traffic. One is a two-lane country road that floods when it rains. The other route, a major four-lane highway, is the most heavily traveled road in the area, specifically before eight o'clock in the morning when everyone is trying to get to work. Instead of exiting at the first exit, where the car manufacturer is located and where thousands are attempting to exit at once, I drive on through the little town and take back roads to my office.

I noticed the freshly mowed field on my left, which was covered in morning dew, and since my window was down, I inhaled the smell of fresh cut grass. As I relished for a moment in that space that transports one through time to fond childhood memories of country living, a flock of crows took flight from the field. As they ascended, I saw squirts of white droppings trailing behind. Since they were headed in the direction of my Jeep, a fear gripped me, not the fear that you might kill one with a car like when a dog rushes out into traffic, but the type that once again the white stuff would be streaked across my hood. I couldn't speed up to avoid them, there were so many, so I slowed down.

People have told me I drive slowly, and I admit that I do drive like an elderly person. I just recently received a letter from my insurance company, giving me an additional ten percent off my annual fees because of my ten-year accident-free record. I am proud of that, even though most folks think it's funny. One co-worker said, "That's great, but you drive like an old man. It's a wonder someone don't run over you." I had responded, "You are just jealous because you don't get that discount." I had a flash from a time when my sister wanted to trade cars with me. I had a Regal and made monthly payments (except the time I spent my checks on the lottery), and she had a twenty-year- old Volkswagen Squareback. I told her I would trade, and she agreed to take over payments. My friends had called me Mr. McGoo. I drove that VW back and forth to work on the interstate with a speed limit of fifty-five. Everyone passed me. In fact, some people gave me dirty looks and blew their horns, and I didn't understand their frustration. After three months, and nearly being run over by a semi on the interstate one day, I told my dad what had been happening. "Didn't your sister tell you the speedometer isn't right? It shows you are doing twenty miles per hour more than you are. So you're really only driving thirty-five miles per hour if it reads fifty-five." I had never felt more embarrassed in my life; however, that didn't last. I received a repossession notice from the bank because payments hadn't been made in three months, so I switched back cars with my sister and caught up on the payments.

Slowing didn't help as the birds circled, and to avoid the

white droppings, I swerved. If anyone has seen crash tests on television, then you know that four-wheel drive vehicles do not take kindly to quick jerks of the wheel. But when you drive like an old man, you apparently don't jerk the wheel quick enough. I did run off the road and into a ditch, but the ditch was shallow, and I managed to get the Jeep back on the road without incident. Cars behind me, however, blew horns and gave me angry looks. These are the same people who tailgate others and speed only to be caught at traffic lights.

When I finally got to work, I was delighted not to have any droppings on my Jeep, but when I left that afternoon, the birds had left me a message. Already too tired from working all day, I decided the birds had won. I vowed I would try not to get so upset over that which I could not control. Of course, I've vowed this before, and it didn't work, but I knew I had to try again.

Genealogy

The most difficult project I have ever undertaken in my life is attempting to discover my roots. I began my project in my college years, and like most people fantasize, I had hoped for some connection to royalty in Scotland, England, Ireland or Wales, but I would have settled for a link to a knight or warrior, even if they weren't the kindest of people. I began the research by asking older relatives and had the notion I would research my dad's line and my mom's line, which would be several lines, actually, since each line doubled with each generation. I met with my maternal grandmother who told me of her parents, farmers, and their parents, farmers, and I was already bored. I asked what they did for excitement, and she told me that the only time life got exciting was when her grandfather came home drunk. (They could hear him coming down the dirt path in the buggy, screaming and shouting.) She said all the grandchildren would take off to the woods and hide until they got a signal from the house that he had passed out. She said he'd point a shotgun at my great grandmother (her mother) and make her play the piano for hours while he slurred songs that in his inebriated mind somehow made sense until he finally slipped into a mumbling mode and then dropped unconscious to the floor. My great grand-mother would keep playing for a while until she was sure he was asleep, and then one of her fifteen siblings would call the younger ones back to the house. My grandmother told me how her grandfather would shoot up the house and furniture when he was drunk, but would then go to town and buy all new furniture the next day because of guilt. She told me how he would jump in the well to try and kill himself and they would pull him out. I wondered why they just didn't let him drown. She told me how he got into an argument with his nephew when they were both drunk, and they shot each other, which is how he finally died. What amazed me most, however, was when she said, "He was a good man."

"Don't you think he was an alcoholic?"

"No, I don't think so. He just liked to drink."

My maternal grandfather's family had come from Ireland, so we were told. They were an industrious, hard-working family with dark reddish skin and dark eyes, and the men mainly worked in the pine woods in turpentine. They would collect the pine resin from trees and distill that into turpentine. Turpentine was used for medicinal cures such as chest rubs, hair treatment for lice, and ingestion for parasites. Their knowledge of turpentine enabled them to distill homemade alcohol for their own consumption and for sale, and word of mouth was their marketing advantage. To disguise their second job, they would sell or trade the homemade brew out of the back of their buggy at the Riverside Primitive Baptist Church, an isolated church nestled within the pine forest. But they only sold the brew after services were over. The church-yard was a peaceful but eerie place, and the graves are not dug as deep as the usual six feet for fear of flooding and caskets floating away.

The image of a deceased loved one moving from his final resting place is a strange one, yet it is more realistic that one might imagine. Once when Julia and I went on a beach trip with friends Shawn and Iris, we discovered this frightening reality. The four of us walked alongside the ocean at Dauphin Island, Alabama. The distant oil rigs off shore took away from the serenity of the retreat, and as Shawn and I scoured the shallows for shells, we stopped to fish out what we thought was a unique shell. The shell was an arm bone, and as I held it, I called out for Iris to identify, since she had a degree in biology. When she confirmed my suspicions, we scanned beneath the murky water and found leg bones and a backbone. Mud-caked clothes rested at the water's edge, and we speculated about a murder or drunken tourist drowning. I dropped the bone back into the water, wondering about the remains of this person, his history. When we reached the pavilion, I saw an officer to whom I tried to explain the situation without seeming like I was guilty of a crime. His matter-of-fact reply astounded me even more than the discovery of human remains: "Happens all the time here. Workers fall off oil rigs or Indian remains wash up after the sea unearths their shell mound burial grounds."

My concern was that if I am buried, I am buried with assurances I won't simply wash away, and I know I won't be buried at Riverside Primitive Baptist Church even though many of my ancestors are. My grandparents had their grave site selected before my grandfather's death. Once when my grandmother went to visit her love's grave to place a new plastic arrangement to replace the once red, then pink and white, poinsettia, she stepped in a hole and fell right onto her future grave, her name on the granite headstone minus her death date. At eighty-something, she could not muster the strength to get up, and she sent her youngest grandchild, who was ten at the time and whom she had been baby sitting, in her car to get help. She watched as the car swerved back and forth, in and out of the sand ruts as he struggled to see over the dashboard. Since the church is isolated, it took a while for him to find help, and all the time she lay atop her grave baking in the Georgia heat.

Switching families, I then investigated my paternal grandmother's family. Again, I found stern Baptists and farmers. Three of my grandmother's siblings had gone blind, and I worried about genetic eye diseases. What relatives told me in whispered voices through cupped hands was that their grandfather, another ancestor who liked to drink but didn't have a drinking problem, got around, caught syphilis as a result of his getting around, and spread it to his wife. His offspring suffered, through no fault of their own. Finally depressed from my illustrious genealogical quest, I decided I couldn't quit until I investigated my paternal grandfather's family, which I thought would have a more promising history. Stories of buried money, a burned plantation house no one knew the origins of anymore, and five thousand acres of land sounded promising. Topping that, four generations are buried at a primitive Baptist church that legends claim is haunted, and it does look eerie with its majestic live oak trees draped in Spanish moss surrounded by only woods. I had been there, toured the land looking for clues, and even toured the remains of a house, where I found tobacco cans from the 1800s behind the chimney. I wanted to use a metal detector and scan the ground for buried money. It was rumored the family buried money and silver when a Civil War skirmish had taken place only a mile away. One generation back was the Scotland connection (via North Carolina, Virginia, or somewhere). My great-great-great grandfather and his three brothers, Revolutionary war heroes with thick Scottish brogues, had arrived after the war, received land grants for their service, and started lives a future descendent would want to go back and live.

Twenty-something years later, several people were still searching for the origins of these mysterious four brothers. One distant cousin had a novel idea. He believed that it was possible that they were not who we had always believed they were. Well, no one wanted to let go of the myth passed down generation after generation. Yet, the more we dug into alternative possibilities, the more circumstantial evidence helped build a case that the four brothers were not, in fact, from Scotland or anywhere in the British Isles, but were descendents of Palatine, or German, immigrants escaping religious persecution and indenturing themselves as servants for the British for passage to Savannah, Georgia. Names like Johann, Appollonia, Maria Barbara, Hans were beginning to replace the English names we had inherited, and had searched for, in every archival record possible. Most importantly, the surname began to crop up in different varieties. It occurred to me that not only did we not know our origins, but we didn't even know what our real name was. Due to language barriers, not illiteracy, the name had been recorded wrong since 1737 when the ship chock full of Germans and Swiss landed at Tybee Island off the coast of Savannah. As I read through colonial records, I read how when the ship docked at Cowes in England, the German-Swiss complained of conditions, particularly the chains, and refused to re-board for the cross-

Atlantic voyage. It was only after an interpreter mediated the situation that the good people settled. Upon arrival, the British lumped them together as Palatines even though some were from Switzerland, France, Austria, and several other areas of Europe. Their names were misrecorded, and they were sent to live in small cabins and given a few supplies to last them. Many died, and actually Darwin's theories proved true—the fittest survived. What finally solidified the case were DNA tests. One fellow, who we knew descended from the German family, had his DNA test conducted, and several of us did as well. A perfect match revealed the truth. Further, another family with a different spelling matched, and no one had known these two families were related for over two hundred years. The whole experience was a shock and required a re-grouping of beliefs and a reorganization of years of research.

Several months turned into two years of work before the circumstantial case proving roots really began to take hold. We learned more about their industriousness: how they worked off their indenture, worked to brick the streets of Savannah, got land grants, began farming operations of several hundred acres, founded mills. Yet we still did not know their origins, and we didn't know their religion. We assume they were Protestant because their future generations were. We didn't know where their graves were because two family cemeteries have only nub Cypress tombstones left from years of weather.

What is most important for those seeking to find roots in the South is to know that the Civil War had a major impact on records. So many courthouses and records have been burned or lost that it's a miracle anyone can find anything at all. What is also important to know is that no matter how big and important people thought they were, they are still dead and go unremembered by many for what they had done while on this planet.

It's quite an eye-opening experience, and yet for all I had learned, and as my wife and I were planning to have our first child, I wanted to know more. I wanted to share with our daughter the truth of our roots. Julia's water broke early in the morning, about four o'clock. The hospital was forty miles away, and though I knew her Volvo would fly, I was still worried about having to help birth a child, for unlike my ancestors, I knew nothing and wanted to keep it that way. I'm a very high-strung person, and when we arrived at the hospital, I expected immediate attention. The admissions clerk, however, was busy eating a bag of Fritos and drinking a Diet Coke. I had often noticed how many people were oblivious to the fact that if they really wanted to lose weight, then they needed to do more than just add Diet Coke to a pathetic diet.

"She is having a baby," I said, pushing my eyebrows together.

"Honey, you need to calm down," she responded, a tiny piece of chewed Frito landing on someone's paperwork. She did waddle to a back room and return, saying "Follow me." I wondered if she would wipe the paperwork, or if someone would get it on his hand later, pick his nose or ear, transfer the chewed particle, and get some disease.

When we entered the birthing suite, it wasn't the hospital rooms I recall from visiting sick relatives as a child. Wooden floors, leather furniture, stylish drapes made the place seem more like a hotel room than a hospital room. The hospital bed, along with the oxygen insert in the wall, and an IV pump on wheels made it seem the right place.

Within a few minutes, nurses were hooking up monitors and sticking IVs in my wife's arm. I was stepping outside, making calls on the cell phone. A couple of hours passed before contractions and pain increased to the point that Julia needed something, and an anesthetist came to give her the epidural. I had heard Julia's friends ask if she was going to get the epidural, and she said she would if she needed to. I thought it was a good idea to inject some medication that would numb the pain of birth. The effects, however, made me wonder if it was worth it or not. As I observed the lumps forming in the back where the needle was inserted, and I watch Julia shake uncontrollably, I wondered what was worse. I kept asking for the doctor, a petite brunette with a model's smile, who seemed very positive and genuine. The nurses said she would be arriving shortly. Words like shortly don't compute when you are watching someone suffer.

Julia's mother arrived and so did her best friend. They were of some comfort, and when the doctor finally showed, it was time. I didn't realize I could stay in the room. Honestly, I didn't want to. I wanted a pill to alleviate the stress and calm my heart rate. I sat in the corner, expressing my concern quietly from time to time while Julia pushed and her mom and friend held her hands and coached. Her mother, who is a nurse, had birthed four children herself, so I figured she knew what to do. The doctor had hundreds of pictures with babies, so I figured she knew what to do, too. I knew nothing and wasn't afraid to admit it. When the doctor reached her hand and part of her arm inside Julia, I had to leave the room, and I wondered why men find watching lesbians exhilarating. Soon, however, as I stood in the hallway, there was an entire medical team on hand. Julia's friend came to get me.

"The baby is stuck in the canal," she said.

"What does that mean?"

"She can't push her out, and she's stressed."

"We're all stressed," I said.

"No, she is in distress; her vital signs are dropping. They need to do an emergency C-section."

My wife had been adamant about not having a C-section. She wanted to give birth naturally, so she wouldn't have a scar. When I darted into the room, the doctor was holding her hand, saying, "We really need to go, Julia. The baby is in danger."

Julia cried and screamed, "No, I don't want a scar."

Everyone looked at me. I said, "Julia, come on. Just have the C-section."

"I'm not," she cried.

Then, the doctor looked at me again. This time, I was louder and more mean-sounding than I had been to the Frito lady. "Just shut up!" I pointed at the medical team who honestly didn't know what to say, clapped my hands together and said, "Take her now. Go."

Before I knew it, they had the tubes, IVs, and the bed all moving down the hall, and Julia was crying. The doctor came out of the surgery room and asked if I wanted to come in. "No, I've seen enough." I told Julia's mother to go, and she did. At least if something happened, she could have helped. While I sat against the wall with Julia's best friend and some other friends who had shown up, a nurse came out to tell me that our daughter, who was now in the world, had meconium in her lungs and they were pumping her lungs; she told us both Julia and the baby were fine, and they were taking the baby to the nursery. In a moment, a screaming infant came rolling through the doors in a glass case on wheels, and I followed behind.

At first, they left her in the case, stuff all over her and her crying, while the nurses stood around talking. Finally, I said, "When are ya'll going to clean her up?" They began to move silently. They wouldn't let me in while they washed her, tagged her, weighed her and so forth, but I watched them through the window. When they finally let me in, I looked at her: pink with small eyes, very little brown hair, and a wide mouth like Julia. She was indeed beautiful, but I noticed our last name was spelled wrong on her bracelet. I told the nurse, "You spelled the name wrong."

"It's no big deal," she snapped.

Now, it's one thing to tell that to anyone off the street, but not to a genealogist. "People have been spelling our name wrong for over two hundred and fifty years," I snapped. "I'll be damned if she's going to come into this world with her name spelled wrong just because someone can't spell. If you don't want to change it, give me a pen, and I'll do it myself."

The nurse walked away, and another nurse got a new bracelet and redid it, and they finally moved her into the room with other babies under a warm light. I stood with a green medical outfit on by her bed and made clucking and chirping sounds to her. She turned her head and looked at me. For the longest time in her infancy, she enjoyed me making sounds like that. Now when I make those sounds, she says, "You're silly, Dada." I think when she's a teen and brings some boys over, I'll do it to them and see what she says.

The next day and those that followed were sweet and relaxing. There was breast- feeding to learn, including pumping. That was a sight to behold, but I knew it had to be done, and I would have to live with it. I was just glad that I didn't have to breast-feed even though I had gained some weight during the pregnancy and had begun to look as if I could. There was learning how to hold her, learning how to change the diaper. The last morning we were there, a nurse came in.

"I understand you do genealogy," she said.

I guess I looked puzzled and wondered if she was a nurse and a psychic. "How do you know that?" I asked.

"Some of the other nurses were talking about your wanting the bracelet changed because they spelled your name wrong."

"Yes, that's true," I said and knew they had been discussing what an ass I was behind my back.

"Some of my family has the same name, and I've been trying to understand the history a bit better."

I explained to her what I knew, what I didn't, and that when I got home I would email her information I had. I spent a lot of time on the computer emailing people and have wondered from time to time what we did before computers, before email. I sent her some information but never heard from her.

Now before my daughter goes to bed at night, we sing songs together—"Down in the Valley", the goodnight song from the Lawrence Welk show (that I resented as a child because there was no cable and it was the only show on Saturday on all three channels), "My Darlin' Clementine," "Old Folks at Home" about the Suwannee River, "Old Suzanna," and others I remember from my own childhood. We say a prayer, and instead of "If I die before I wake, I pray to the Lord my soul to take," we say, "May angels watch me through the night until I wake in morning light" because of the lack of sleep I would get as a child thinking I would die. I wonder if thinking angels are watching would affect sleep, but I'll bet not as much as dying would. I tell her stories about our wonderful ancestors who came here, so they could live free. I hate that they are not completely true, since I still don't know much about them, but maybe it will inspire her and now her little brother, who was born two years later, to desire to learn more about their roots, or at least, appreciate history. His birth, incidentally, wasn't nearly as complicated, though Julia did have to have a C-section, and since I hadn't seen my daughter come into the world, I felt I should at least experience it. Though it seemed rather traumatic to me, with the doctors and nurses tugging and pulling skin until they had him out, I was rather pleased that the first thing he did when they held him up was urinate on them. There was some justice there, I thought, and I imagine our ancestors would have been proud.

ABOUT THE AUTHOR

Born in 1964 in Valdosta, Georgia, Niles Reddick grew up in the small town of Hahira, Georgia. He graduated from Valdosta State University with a B.A. in Philosophy, State University of West Georgia with a M.A. in Psychology, and Florida State University with a Ph.D. in Humanities and an emphasis in English and Literature. His dissertation, *Eccentricity as Narrative Technique*, included interviews with Lee Smith, Clyde Edgerton, and Janice Daugharty.

Reddick taught English and Psychology at Thomas University in Thomasville, Georgia, and Georgia Military College at Moody AFB, Georgia, before accepting an English teaching position at Motlow College in Lynchburg, Tennessee. At Motlow, he coordinated the Writer's festival and secured such renowned writers as Michael Lee West, Manette Ansay, Jerry Bledsoe, and Sharyn McCrumb. He also served as Editor of *The Distillery* for two years, taking the journal from a regional publication to an international one distributed by Ingram and one that received recognition and acclaim from *The Literary Magazine Review* and *Library Journal*.

Most recently, Reddick is the Dean of Humanities and Social Science for Motlow College and serves as a free-lance editor. He is on the editorial board for *Honors in Practice,* a journal published by the National Collegiate Honors Council. Reddick lives in Murfreesboro, Tennessee, with his wife Michelle, and children Audrey and Nicholas, and dog Harper Lee, named for the author.

For your reading pleasure, we invite you to visit our web bookstore

WHISKEY CREEK PRESS

www.whiskeycreekpress.com